Copyright © 2019 Suiyi Tang
All rights reserved.
Typesetting by Janice Lee
Copyediting by Esa Grigsby
Cover Design by Dawn Wu
Special Thanks to Devyn Radke
ISBN 978-1-948700-98-6

THE ACCOMPLICES:
A #RECURRENT Book

theaccomplices.org

THE ACCOMPLICES

AMERICAN SYMPHONY: OTHER WHITE LIES

BY SUIYI TANG

PREFACE

she thought long and hard about how she might begin
this book. after all, how does one go about completing
their last words? usually, it was a spontaneous affair,
uttered in those last moments, which, if one was lucky,
were spent under the watchful eye of loved ones. last
words: a final performance, as it were. but she had little
such luck, for, in the long course of the play that was her
life, she had rehearsed the farewell scene one time too
many, so that when the actuality of death approached,
she found that there were no audience members left. she
didn't mind, however; whatever last words she had were
already spoken. still, the last moments of her life, spent
in obscurity, would be lost to the world forever as its sole
witness escaped with the Event. but it was a disappearing
act until the very end, for it was only the illusion of
disappearance that her (presumed) death wrought; there
are speculations as to whether or not she is truly gone.
had she known that more parts of her remained than the
actress's coy grin, she might have taken liberties to prepare
her body, or assert with more fervor her last address. as it
turned out, she did not know, so it is at the base of closed
curtains that we read this curt introduction:

AMERICAN SYMPHONY: OTHER WHITE LIES

for a long time, i was unsure how to lay my body down to rest. should i ease onto my back, letting the ceiling overwhelm me until sleep, or deliriousness, came? or should i stifle whatever tormenting thoughts were keeping me with the cotton mesh of pillow? perhaps it was simpler than that—a single unfolding, so that flesh could hang from bone, and the spirit unhinge itself from the body. these works were begat from this question of how the body might lay, and in doing so, evacuate itself. but enough with nonsense. this work is about form, and auto/meta/fiction as a means of looking back at the inscrutable body, to create a reflection for moments in which the mirror fails us.

but don't mistake it for my encore! that, dear Reader, is yet to come. for now, this is all that you may take of me.

TO NADJA, WHEREVER SHE MAY BE—MAY HER LEGACY OVERSHADOW THAT OF HER CREATOR

INTRODUCTION: A EULOGY FOR !, or, as she referred to herself, S and ?

for my part, i, too, have thought long and hard about how to begin this book. after all, how does one go about preparing the resting body of someone they barely knew? luckily, the nature of knowledge, a retrospective acquisition, is anachronistic. if i didn't think i knew ! then, i certainly do now. what remains of her once voluminous troves of costumes are the following pages: a short lifetime's worth of frills and loose ends, which she and i have compiled together, for your sake, and hers. i am a believer of death's dignity, and in order for dignity to exist, the deceased must be presented as she might have wished, even if there is no one to see it; even if she is no longer there herself. many months ago, i set about completing this last favor to S.

i still remember the night we met—it was a muggy evening, typical of those late summers in berkeley. a mutual friend had hosted a party and convinced !, still fresh from her disastrous stint at college, to attend. i found her on the balcony, smoking from a glass bong the size of her face, clad in a stunning black number from which her sleek limbs tumbled in knots. even with the refraction of the pipe, which enlarged half of her face to comical effect, she was striking. later, she told me she had found me likewise magnetic.

it was a friendship shadowed by infinite erotic possibilities. though many of our mutual friends thought us a couple (mistaking intimacy for the illusion of sex), we never bothered to correct them. sex threatened to bring us too dangerously close, thus shattering the filmy phantasms we had created of the other. in the absence of protection, we refrained. in retrospect, i think the real reason we deprived ourselves of that singular satisfaction was this: we sensed, in the other, a penetrating gaze that threatened to undo the boundaries of the self. only now, after she has gone, can i say with certainty that though she resigned herself to the limitations of the border, she never abandoned the desire for largesse. instead, she has left me with the resources to know her as she once wished to be known, with more clarity than perhaps even she herself possessed.

after that fall, S disappeared again, to travel, or so she said, and we kept only sparse contact from that point on. it was then that the time between us seemed to collapse along a sticky string. i learned many details of her life long after she exited mine, and there are many details that i am sure i will never know (those who may know, may God bless them). i did not know, for example, the number of ways her body could contort itself, producing startling portraits from whose frames only her shadow peered. then, as before, i could not look away.

when i found out about her final disappearance to date, i was shocked, but not entirely surprised. ! had a way of finding herself in situations she did not intend, and it was precisely this quality of spontaneity that allowed me to love, but never completely trust, her. i suppose i was right, for it is never wise to trust someone who will one day disappear on you.

for months afterward, i was tormented by nightmares. always gruesome, starring the death of a young girl who i could never be sure was her. those violent reenactments, suppressed by the light of day, continued to find a way to me, trailing screen to streets so that long after the nightmares stopped, i was jerked into an anxious wakefulness at even the thought of her. so much for disappearance.

evidently, i was not the only one grieving her, but i was, as it turned out, the only one brave enough to broach the boxes she left behind. she had not much of an artistic legacy at that point, and her peers, alternately jealous and mournful, felt it unfit to open the pandora's box of her ashes. her parents, cautious of what they might find (to the detrimental effect of their daughter's value, in their eyes at least), handed the scraps to me with little hesitation. they trusted me, or saw my intent was benevolent; that i sought not to excavate her, but to offer her a chance at farewell. be kind to her, her father had said to me by way of parting.

so she came to stay with me, or what was left of her, anyway. as a way of relieving the horrors of the imagination, i had at first sought to confront her by assembling her into an archive, and in doing so, remembering some of the bountiful warmth she possessed. unsurprisingly, as i dug deeper, i found not only a still-warm body, but *her*, again— that flinty soul i had fallen in love with all those years ago. slightly more refined, with a newfound penchant for cynicism, but the same foundational essence nonetheless. there was something infinitely comforting about retracing those alleys through which she had once taken me, only now, in the absence of a guide, i was left to don one of her many masks and lead myself, following her still-visible footprints. in that way, i received double the reassurance— of not only receiving her once more, but filling her ghost with my own body. the effect was an immediacy that, long ago, we had simultaneously yearned for and despised.

in these pages, you will find a portrait of her making. as i am, foundationally, a voyeur, this work is less mine than it is hers. if i could, i would eschew even the semblance of authorship for the station of witness, for i am as much an audience as you, though perhaps i know my way around the smoke screen a little better. but it is of no matter. the miscellaneous effects she has left—letters, diary entries, unfinished projects, endless ear-marked pages and inadvertent scrapbooks—speak for themselves, which is to say, for her. she knew the danger of the abandoned document, how the wiles of circulation distorted even the purest of original intentions. i do not think she left these traces behind so we could forget them: rather, they form a context of their own, tracing the rough outline of her psyche to form a last refrain of her life's work.

a single manuscript lines the exception of her scattered parts. titled AMERICAN SYMPHONY, this minor publication is the only full work of hers that exists, which i have included in the following pages. in its wake, i feel less a mediator than a guardian. after all, how do you give voice to a woman who already has one? what she needed in these last words was not me, but a certainty of form, whose illusion of freedom could animate the rich effects she had buried. i set about laying the groundwork for this mélange of queer objects, heeding her father's request to be kind, but feeling that, in certain contexts, brutality was its own form of kindness—hers and mine. she would have liked it a little unpolished, i think, as perfection remained the one ruse from which she ran all her life. in death, as in life, the truth, as she might have told it. i have only one regret, which is never having asked her if she trusted me. i like to think that she did, but with regard to the affective truth, the only one that mattered, it is up to these pages to do their work. she was much too buoyant to be buried.

–SYT
november, 2048

table of contents

part I: the blue

diary entries (editor's note: undated)

[1]

    after my suicide (attempt), i left school and relocated to berkeley, california. i don't want to live in berkeley, i complained to my friend S. i don't want to become that bitch. S looked at me, unimpressed. do you own birkenstocks, she asked. i nodded. and your parents, a house. nod, again. is it true that you possess two closets and three pairs of doc martens, and consider yourself to be a member of the upper middle class. i looked at her. you are already that bitch, she said.

    my mother was worried that i would be too lonely in berkeley, and, left to my own devices, actually commit (this time) to something else of equal stupidity. she called me often, cajoling me about what i was doing, or lack thereof. our conversations took the same turns: what do you have planned today, pause. have you seen any friends, pause. the dog is constipated again, and had an accident in your father's shoe. my mother kept the same schedule, toggling the park, ranch 99, and her doctor's office with a kind of content consistency that made me alternately depressed and relieved. under her persuasion, i signed up for yoga class, buying a seventy-dollar rubber mat with her credit card. i got a babysitting job and medical marijuana card in rapid succession. three times a week, i woke up early and made my way to the city for work, then stumbled back to berkeley and pretended to work on a book. i pretended to do a lot of things: earning money, writing, stretching my spine in downward dog. despite (or because of) what i told myself, my life took on a routine and began to resemble that of a sane person's.

not long after i got settled in, A got in touch. we had been rivals in high school, alternately friendly and fiercely cruel in a petty auction to outdo the other as the loudest, most arrogant pseudo-intellectual of our suburban purgatory. by the beginning of senior year, we ran the model united nations club together, and everyone was convinced we were either dating or related (a spiritual relation that transcended our obvious physical differences). A was now a junior in college, the same he'd always been, he said, just funnier. he invited me to a labor day party, to be held in the house he shared with some debate friends. i arrived a full twenty minutes early, tightly wound by a late-afternoon cup of coffee that i had chugged to stave off my hesitation. while i stood in line at the grubby starbucks on shattuck, a chinese boy tapped me on the shoulder.

are you ---? i looked at him, and considered lying. oh, i know you from ---, he said, sliding the name of my ex-school the way one would hermés, or andover, or uptown. i took pleasure in the fact that i was unable to recall ever meeting him. i considered asking him how he knew me, but before i could, he laugh-spat and told me that i sure had a way of getting around. my cheeks flushed, and then rang. i wondered if he was a late-night mistake, or a member of my personal execution squad, or quite possibly, both. i drank my coffee and looked out the smeared window while he mansplained our school's newest ranking in usa today.

when i arrived at A's house (finally, but not late enough), he was not home. this was typical A, who checked his text messages as a pregnant person might their period tracker. (i think A might be the only person the national security agency might one day have trouble locating.) his housemates were still getting ready for the party, evidenced by the tepid r&b playing on their stereo. i was given a beer and allowed to watch them pour vodka into a fruit bowl. sometime later, when i began to feel the alcohol and was considering retiring to the porch with my joint, A showed up. panting, he ran a hand through his hair and immediately set to the fridge for a bite to eat. my attempts at enthusiasm were not returned, but he turned to his friends, and with a queer little smile, introduced me as an "old friend from high school." do you want a hit, i asked A, i think i'm going to go smoke on your balcony, if that's okay. nah, he replied, and though i wasn't sure which question he was answering, i decided to chastely look the other way. ok, i said. i'll be on the balcony.

the rest of the party passed in a blur. at some point, i was joined by a bong, and a steady trickle of smokers who wandered out to take a break from the party inside. finally relaxed, and proffering weed for conversation, i became the unofficial guardian of the smoke station, a position which i continued for some while. out of nowhere, A showed up, clearly a little drunk, with a girl at his arm. ---! he called out, using the name i had discarded since high school. you have to meet S. to be honest, i don't remember those first lines of exchange between S and myself (two S's! how serendipitous, i must have remarked). she said something calm and self-actualized like, that's a big bong you got there, and i replied with something witty, i'm sure. before i knew it, we were smoking away and drowning out everyone else at the party.

[2]

the first crash came when i stepped off the bus. the sky, a swirl of greys and off-whites, as if an opaque parallel of the pooling cement below. construction blocked off the road leading into the condominium complex where i was staying, and machinery, pregnant with the still-wet of fresh mud, gazed upward. but it was a thunderstorm with all of the props and none of the actuality. is a thunderstorm still a thunderstorm if there is no rainfall? shuddering without the expectant release. thunder, like the itch of an aborted sneeze. walking toward my room, above which grey clouds concentrated, as if an epicenter of the not-yet-storm. (it did not strike me then that this could also have been the aftermath of an already-there-storm. all the evidence pointed to this possibility: the already-wet ground, the silence which stretched between the claps, the moist paper bag which i clutched under one arm.)

it was only after i came out of the shower, hair dripping noisily down silent tiles, that i convinced myself the storm had passed. under the hallucination of thunderclouds, the hallway took on a chiaroscuro quality that felt cool-blue and echoed, as if silence could sound. i have always been drawn to ground zeroes and the soundless terrain that succeeds them— counterfactuals and the shudder that interrupts a would-be quiet. though blue would seem to promise the clarity of a sunny tomorrow, and even the memory of a stormless yesterday, i no longer believe in such things as "calm," and "after." but i continue to mourn for counterfactuals. such as: hair washed with rainwater, or roads that dissolve even though there is no storm.

perhaps because i have been living in such a blue space myself, i can no longer tell the difference between colors or the vibration that precedes them. only hues of blue, which light up the precise locations of where i have been and where i am to go. which is why, when it was time for me to commit to the act of dying, i could not take even that final breath of dignity. little blue pills do not blue blood spill. but, byzantium births palatinate, iris, and so on, until all blood cells turn the purplish-blue of a bruise, or capillaries clotted with hemoglobin starved of oxygen. they say that the color blue emits calmness, i think, like the blue of ice, the silence of glaciers, the muffled crash of bodies bruised by a sinking sea. "if all human hemoglobin were free in the plasma rather than being contained in red blood cells, the circulatory fluid would be too viscous for the cardiovascular system to function effectively." what if freedom and immobility—the frozen breath—were but two sides of the same coin?

one must commit to suicide, but i could not take even that final breath of dignity. so i think to myself, curled on that springy mattress the color of deep calm, a sea of capillaries spilling from my arms. my stomach anchored itself deeper into the iris waves, until jellyfish bubbled from acid and what used to be flesh grew itchy with a second skin of barnacle. when i arrive at the bottom of the ocean floor, leaking blue, i found that i could not bring myself to sit with the silence of the vibrations. instead, murky eyes continued to gaze into the foci of the horizon, transmogrifying the landscape into more palatable animations of what i already knew. it was then that i realized the qualifier "blue blooded" is but a misnomer: blood was not really blue, but a palatinate shade that resembled bruises. a language of explanations can only ache, and never touch. the only language of leaking capillaries, or what it would feel like to swim in hemoglobin. thus frozen, i found not release, but suspension.

보호해줘야 한대. 천연 기념물이라고
He has to be protected, since he is a minor object.

Personal information

serum

S considered all the ways that she could lie to her father's friend. when the text had come, at eight in the previous evening, she had glanced at her phone with the distaste one might reserve for an ex, or a brother, or, at worst, a mother. "we would like to invite you over to our house for christmas eve dinner at six pm," the message read. she knew her father had gone out of his way to reach out to his friend, another portly man in his fifties, and that in all consideration she should show face for the sake of being polite. yet she had already made up her mind not to go. it was only when her mother phoned the following day, reminding her that she had yet to respond to the family friend's query, that S paused to give thought to the brief message. as she mulled over to respond with a delicacy that verged indistinguishably between polite and cold, her phone rang. it was the friend's daughter, a broad-shouldered girl still in her junior year of high school. S had met her on two other occasions, to both parties' awkward disappointment. she had found the girl dull, evincing a mind yet unopened but bubbling with inane questions, to which she had no good answers. though she was none the wiser, S's verbose meditations on philosophy had seemed, to the opposite party, alternately arrogant and full of an incomprehensible folly that convinced the young girl that a humanities degree was truly useless. the phone rang again, and S unscrupulously pressed ignore. *provincial*, S thought to herself, grimacing at the girl's audacity to phone, with a dumb insistence that echoed her questions. like father, like daughter.

it was not a very charitable thought, but of those, S had few. since her suicide attempt earlier that spring, she found herself incapable, in her internal monologue, to entertain little besides a passive-aggressive deluge of self-pity. she alternated between debilitating insecurity and an inexplicable anger that she (wrongly) attributed to a lingering neurochemical imbalance. the throes of S's silent tantrum produced no visible marker, save a small wart beneath her left eye which seemed to grow, to her distress, in direct correlation to her surmounting sourness, making her look simultaneously like a diseased wench and a downtrodden witch. she rubbed at her eye nervously.

she had read an article about a man whose unwashed pillowcases had resulted in a mite infestation on his eyelashes, with as many as ten mites clinging to each lash when he, forced by a sudden and violent eye infection, finally reported to the hospital. S rubbed her itchy eyes. she visualized a mite colony growing on her lids, their tiny, worm-like bodies engorging en masse, and shivered with irritation. in her vanity, she had recently begun to rub castor oil on her lash line before bed every night, hearing that it would stimulate eyelash growth. S had always been somewhat ashamed of her prickly eyelashes, whose already infantile presence were made virtually nonexistent by her inward-folded eyelids. she rubbed her eyes again, and twitched at the next vibration of her phone. it was the broad-shouldered high schooler, again. S hit "ignore," and typed out a polite message accepting the offer. thus, a momentary lapse of judgement, triggered by the growing crack in her psyche, resulted in S's attendance the next evening.

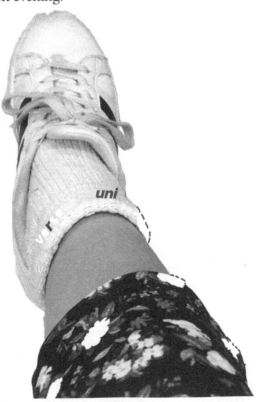

S's hair, cut short and dyed a metallic grey, was met with mild praise from the friend's family. even the broad-shouldered girl, ignorant though she was, remarked that it seemed very stylish. like you'd know, S thought perniciously, as the pressure beneath her left eye mounted. it was, by all accounts, a scurrilously consumed dinner, seasoned with backhanded compliments and sardonic double-meanings. despite her usual cynicism, S felt ill at ease. pushed together by the collective will of their fathers, she and the broad-shouldered girl endured their time together, tiring the usual cycles of small talk. to her credit, the broad-shouldered girl seemed, each time, powered by a sincerity that embarrassed S and made her wonder about the provenance of ignorance. S was unsure if she was to feel sorry for the girl's utter lack of self-awareness, or angered by her willful ignorance regarding anything to do with culture, history, or the arts. no such pettiness bothered the other party, it seemed, who cheerily probed S to explain, once more, everything from her hobbies to the last thing she ate. scarcely did she understand this queer creature, whose rapid speech and indignant repose set her apart from anyone else the broad-shouldered girl knew. it must be an american thing, her parents had mused, by way of explanation; america, that strange land, who mothered a kind of perversity, as was evident in this grey-haired girl. it fascinated and frightened her. for her part, S became quickly annoyed with the girl's attention, which she felt performed a kind of sticking and sliding that made her feel like a slice of melting cake, being consumed as unceremoniously (albeit slightly disgustingly) as one would sickeningly sweet dough. S knew her idiosyncrasies were alluring to the commonplace, yet, equally as she delighted in the exorbitance of flattery, she despised fascination, and by greater heights of abhorrence, the probing gaze of desire, which cast her as an object of unknowable difference. she was thus ensconced in her steady avoidance of eye contact when she was startled by the broad-shouldered girl's sudden pause. what? S asked. does your, um hair, the girl said, her vowels latching together in a lilt, represent some kind of message? what? S asked again. do you design your appearance, for instance, the girl said more confidently, having gained some momentum at S's expense, to make some sort of statement? what do you mean, S replied. realizing that her entire body had, by this point, steadily turned further away from the broad-shouldered girl, S consciously reoriented her knees back toward the girl. well, the girl said, carefully, and leaned in, does your appearance attempt to make some sort of statement or provoke, like, gender neutrality, or something? the strange excitement in her voice stopped S. she gazed at the girl for a beat, and answered simply, yes. there was no doubt, to S's trained ear, that her hair, so innocuous had it been to her, whose futch experimentation rarely garnered a side-glance by more daring faeries and androgynous dykes, was not so to the broad-shouldered girl. S regarded her for another moment, and deliberately shifted her seat away. in that moment, she saw in the girl an unawakened eroticism, dulled by ignorance and permanently muted by willful stupidity, that incurred a curdling sense of déjà vu. immediately, S felt the unwelcome blush of shame, and she felt a mixture of pity and disgust for the girl, who, for all her plainness and sincere platitudes, remained so antagonistic to everything out of the ordinary—indeed, everything S stood for— that she could not help but become aroused by those very symbols to which she had assigned perversity.

the idea occurred to her during a dream. it had been nestling there for several days, curled in her subconscious like a tight-lipped fern, before unfurling one night as she fell asleep to the blue glow of the computer screen. she dreamt with a clarity rarely afforded to her waking hours, until she found herself looking forward to the night with a vivacity she had never felt for the day. she had read somewhere that in dreaming, the subconscious mimics the elaborate process of a theater, scripting, filming, and playing hundreds of features every night. in this extended allegory, she was simultaneously director, writer, actor, and viewer, and none of them at all, or something else entirely—the very spirit of a schizophrenic gestalt. she found in herself a palimpsest of dialogues; like a solipsistic symphony, each note created by an instrument of her invention, every vibration thrilling her unique psycho-sexual needs. in dreaming, her characters became sharper versions of the ones she met in daylight, imbued with (even she had to admit) well-written dialogue and thrilling turns of events that echoed the unpredictable logic of life so exactly that they became more accurate than life itself every night, she closed her eyes with anticipation, as if eagerly settling in to a new episode of her favorite soap, or looking forward to her *real* life. never did it occur to her to keep a dream journal, for, she found, despite their immersive cinematography and high definition viewing experience, the films of her subconscious played in a theater reserved only for her, and immediately lost the luster of reality when she attempted to articulate them to waking audiences.

one night, she dreamt that she was a grey-haired witch, and awoke touching her hair, surprised to find it the length and timbre she had left it before falling asleep. still unbelieving, she rubbed her sleep-filled eyes and stroked her licorice locks, remembering the short bristles they had been mere minutes before. that day, she took the bus downtown, and checked into a mid-tier hair salon with chains across the city. she could have gone anywhere, but her anticipatory anxiety chose this: she asked for a quote, and instructed the stylist to lop her hair and dye it the color of faded starlight.

diary excerpts

fri, jan 26

woke up at five this morning. ate a light breakfast (no coffee!) and answered some emails until seven; dawdled a bit more, and was out of the apartment by nine. hotel is wonderful—my room overlooks an intersection of carrer d'aribau, a meeting of three streets by barcelona's famed barrio del eixample. i live in one of those grand modernist giants, and by morning can see straight down the cobbled streets to the university, over the comforting din of traffic. quite romantic.

after breakfast, took a gummy (approx 10:00 a.m.) and headed to picasso museum, where i stayed until past 2:00 p.m., drinking in the rich legacy of catalonia's most famous painter. how versatile the man was; his works evince an awkward grace which, upon closer examination, belies a masterful relation to primary colors and an exquisite brushstroke (one that extended into the arches of the copper etching). considered the chronic disruption of cubist assemblage; abstraction + time; picasso's pornographic gaze and altogether marvelous (if exceedingly masculinist) effect of his works. saw through the entire (very crowded) museum, and left with 30 euros worth of prints.

lunch at els quatre gats, that famed relic of barcelona's modernist renaissance. lunch was mediocre and expensive— spent 40 euros on two tapas and a sangria which i couldn't finish. another failed pursuit of reenactment, but the cafe's interior was charming.

came down from my high, and felt suddenly exhausted. returned to the room around four and slept until 8:30 p.m., then to un concierto de guitarra. closing act, a piece by lorca (who knew he composed text of this variety)! santa maria del pi, with makeshift stage set on altar—ironic, but playful, and i was ultimately won over by performer's humorous display.

she found herself, with great trepidation, in awe and fear of the world around her. she had surprised herself with her desire to run, or stay hidden as a voyeur shielded by paranoia. her flight instinct was strong, and, paired with a tepid imagination of the erotic (to whose credit her shameful absolution could be attributed), she saw the world as a zero-sum game, her face the marble piece with which she played. i'll pay for this, she thought often, almost irrationally stricken to fright at the sight of a misplaced shoe; sudden ember-persistent ashes. or was it that her world, with its endless calculations and ungraspable sums, was in fact the greatest ruse of them all: a marketplace of diminishing returns, kept at bay by her frightened repose.

sat, jan 27

woke up at 8:30 a.m., out the door by 9:50 a.m. to coffee and then the museum of contemporary art, where i stayed until past 2:00 p.m. wonderful exhibit on the (anti-)poems of joan brossa. a notable bit curated around surfaces—minimalism (+ its post-) and art noveau. latifa echakhch had a striking piece titled "with every stencil a revolution"—visceral splatters of blue paint (international klein blue) and faded violet on a wall plastered with the paper of political pamphlets favored by revolutionaries from london to libya. from my notes: "violence incurred in the blue space [melancholic holding place], as if battle had been frozen and then sterilized." notable quote by rauschenberg, paraphrased: artist is another material in the work. the work: transgressing limitations of representation to become the Real itself. the extension of surrealist ideation.

after a quick lunch, to la sagrada familia—gaudí's art nouveau-infused biomimicry is a feat on the levels of aesthetic and ecumenical reinterpretation, stylistically and technically ahead of his time. the basilica, an assemblage wrought through an endless century, long ago expected to be finished in 1926. signs of incongruity, interruptions evident in facade and interior decorations. gaudí may have attempted a modernist transformation of Body of Christ to transcendent Man (an originary space pure as eden) but the result is more an outwardly turned rhizome. fun fact: the exterior of the church bears sculptures of infants made from the casts of dead babies. tour guide: not ironic, but accidentally inspiring—the infant martyrs killed in search of jesus; for this reason, and the symbolic purposes of new life, infants are sacred. i can never figure out the christian church.

sun, jan 28

mass at la sagrada familia. scrambled points of contact between the congregation made more frenetic by the organist's erratic leg movements, whose pumping appeared both energetic and belabored from afar. i believe in divinity and divine spaces. that which is divine is also subject to sacrilege, a thought which gives me considerable anxiety as it reminds of the perpetual edge on which one stands. i am writing to rid myself of this anxiety—filled to the brim with a sense of anticipatory rupture. ignorance of its direction leaves me stranded in the track of the guillotine, twitching at constant anticipation of the shock. how to worry, when there is nothing to worry about and the world at stake? i have left my trusty moleskin at home. there is no possibility of consultation, so i am left in this city, alone despite the amorous excess of vacationing couples and catalonian trills.
strange to me that i still can't let go of the singapore in my dreams. singapore, of my dreams—lying between and betwixt the boundaries of my desire and their unmet

possibilities. writing this in a posh laundromat, whose sleekness reminds me of singapore's most ardent public relations facade. but the man next to me lisps in a tongue unbecoming of the sharp singaporean lilt i have come to associate with...thunderstorms, click-clack of kitten heels, the oeuvre of bluntness singaporeans take for granted about themselves.

twelve more minutes to go. catalonians, on the whole, are open and amicable. today on the subway, a little old lady tapped me on the shoulder, pointed to the napkins spilling out from the side of my bag, and gestured to me that i should close the strap, lest a pickpocketer try his luck. nothing much here, i wanted to tell her, but, trapped by the ignorance of my tongue, i gave her a sweet smile instead. just earlier, a greying man showed me how to operate the laundry machines, catching me as i mistakenly began to load my things into a machine meant for extra weight. i am grateful for these small kindnesses. i miss singapore with the desperation of a rotten lover, unable to articulate the finer points of my desire, which seem to shimmer and disappear as i approach, leaving me to question if, indeed, it is the Little Red Dot that i miss, or something else entirely in its shadow. try as i might, i can't recall the claustrophobia i know i felt during my last days there. only—sunlight, safety, the brimming mark of closeted potentials. i hope this yearning will lead me somewhere warm.

from bolaño: "it was an abyss without monsters, holding only darkness, silence, and emptiness, three extremes that caused me pain, a lesser pain, true, a flutter in the stomach, but a pain that sometimes felt like fear."

after georges méliès, dislocation mystérieuse

S sat slumped over the desk, concerned about her mounting cigarette habit. the urge had arrived to step onto the balcony and light another marlboro. the thought of a slow death was comforting; her participation in its actualization felt deliberate. she thought of joan didion: "we tell ourselves stories in order to live." the best stories were deliberate affairs, every groove rounded to fit in perfect concert with the other. but most stories could not achieve such perfection; most stories jutted and bent with the inconsistency of an emotional hypochondriac. it was safe to assume that a happy accident was the sole source of any momentary shimmer most stories provided. were it not for the persistent goodwill of their authors, most stories would never be published. but all fiction eventually failed—it was designed to do so, lest its readers become mesmerized by the sheer fabric of an impossible world, to the tune of quixotic irreverence (no, we can't have that). rarely, in the presence of the truly sublime story (such as that of gide, or cocteau, or the postmortem contemporary junot díaz), she would glower darkly to herself, knowing that despite narratological brilliance and a quivery sensitivity to language, those fictions, too, would fail. it is unclear who fails whom.

a month ago, she finally began reading *a thousand plateaus*. she woke, convinced that if fictions were a means of world-making, theory was the cynic's attempt at imagination. she told such inventions of how and why and where, not in order to live, but because she could not choose otherwise. a singular promise of truth lies behind the psychological impetus of the propaganda machine; as its delusional documentarian, she wove explanations in place of truth. so that the world may be more palatable, as if impossible feats grew smaller in the light of revelation. faced with such false dichotomies as articulation and actualization, deleuze and guattari chose the route of the cartographical. knowing that the construction of the known would lead to anticipations of the yet-to-be-known gave her great astuteness in her currency of multisyllabic tête-à-têtes. despite the sticky excess of labyrinthine vowels and anticipatory nothings, there would always be a way out, another way to fail with deliberate ecstasy.

a month ago, she awoke, unable to walk down the street. her fingers simply would not work, by which i mean, they refused to stay attached to her knuckles, or her palms, or even her wrists. she had no idea whether her heart still existed, and if so, where it might be. the last time she had felt the thump-thumping of its reassurance was in nagasaki, where, over tilled mountains and art deco houses, she had felt something like the touch of narrative coherence. but nagasaki was a place riddled with the potholes of history, undeterred by the singular drive toward destruction which paved the possibility of its blue existence (sterile, with an inability to produce artifact; heavy, with clouds unable to abort the moisture of their recess). she had felt some identification with the place, with its distorted trees and fresh concrete. if you squint your eyes, you could almost forget that you were gliding amongst corpses.

corpses, those were what she stuffed in the tattered canvas bags when she longed for solitude. she imagined the solidity of a still body, its density unyielding to change even as the effects of decay multiplied. the static commitment of a corpse bespoke either a stoic grace or asinine denial. even in death, the body heeded a will of its own. but on this particular day, her body would not heed any will, gently disassembling as it were. no matter how loud she screamed, she could not put the pieces back together again. elsewhere they floated, attaching themselves to the sides of buildings, the backs of cars, and, in the case of the wriggling tongue, the very bottom of a bystander's shoe, writhing as it wedged its way between sole and soil.

★★★

they termed the qualifier "blue-blooded," it was not really blue that they were after, but the palatinate shade of bruises, or, pills starved into words that never stop explaining.

but when i arrive, i find that i cannot bring myself to sit with the stillness of ground zero. instead, i hike concrete hills and continue to gaze into the foci of the horizon. transmogrifying the landscape into more palatable animations of what i already knew.

He was sitting on the velvet couch in the lobby of the conference hotel when he saw her. Cup to his lips, he caught a glimpse of maroon and the loping stride which, though he had known intimately for not three months, he could never forget. He lowered his cup. The owner of the dress, her face partially obscured by the extravagant frill of the collar, was a gaunt woman bedecked with bruise-colored lips. As if feeling his gaze, she stopped, glanced half-heartedly in his direction, and lowered her eyes to the translucent phone in her hand. She was talking now, her neck bent at an angle, jutting awkwardly (and, he thought, sensuously) from the petal of her bosom. He looked away. This was not the silver-haired girl he had known, though, in the many years after their unfateful meeting, he had come to know many silver-haired girls, each an abbreviation of the first. he remembered the thick sweetness of those lips, the wisp of hair, gold in the candlelight, and looked up. The woman met his gaze. Her eyes, lined imperceptibly with rouge in the likeness of her dress, widened. He noted that she still had the same chin, a soft affair which stretched into wavy locks now a jet-black. The overflowing quality of her hair narrowed her face pleasingly, and gave her a quality of innocence which he had not remembered. She opened her mouth.

"João?" she walked over to him. He could her the soft taps of her shoes, the ropy musculature of calf rising to meet the dark curve of her thigh. He stood, and made to smile. She stopped three feet short of him, neck still extended. "Is that really you?"

He laughed quietly. "Yes, S. And is it really you?" He leaned toward her, but, as if anticipating his action, she took a step forward and embraced him. They looked at each other. He noted, somewhat consciously, her enumerating gaze. Physically, he had not changed much. His once wiry body had rounded a touch, his cheeks had grown a little sallower, but the boyish brown hair she had once adored remained the same. She looked in his eyes, drinking him in.

"What are you doing here?" he asked. In her heels, she rose slightly above him, and he tilted his head to return her gaze.

"Oh," she turned her wrist (the same gentle flamboyance he remembered), "Not much." There was a pause. "My husband is presenting on the risk assessment panel. I just tagged along—Lisbon, you know. I have such fond memories here, and it's been so long since I've been back."

She spoke softly, but beneath the lyrical lilt of her sentences he sensed a familiar vivacity of speech. In the face of discomfort, she talked to fill the silence—this had to be true then as well, he remembered that much. He thought suddenly of the nights they had spent, fucking quietly in her rented bedroom with only the squeaking of the ancient bedframe and her stifled sigh in his ear. There was a time when he would have been aroused, but the long shadows of the years had wilted youthful vigor into a chiaroscuro tainted with melancholy.

"And you?" she was still looking at him.

"On behalf of the government," he smiled wanly. "The forum on inflationary risk. After the financial crisis…"

The edge of her lip turned upward in a half-smirk. "So I see," she said. "You are ever the economist, after all."

He smiled faintly. She chuckled, a gentle cajole. "And the fearless spirit of revolt?" Such empty language of revolution had come easily to them both.

"The natural order of things," he replied. He wondered how much of him she still remembered. How disillusionment had molded this woman before him into a creature of convention, he could not fathom. She could be anyone—a businesswoman, a mistress, an hostess at the hotel, dressed to seduce the pockets of a suit more expensive than his. "And your husband, what does he do?"

She rolled her eyes, then smiled at him playfully. "God knows. Well, you know. The business of identification."

He lifted an eyebrow, and she, in turn, puckered her lips. "I teach, now. English, can you believe it? No tenure, yet, but my husband, he keeps saying—they don't want publication, just his money." She laughed softly. "How offensive. Though it's certainly true, I bear less of a burden with him on the Board of Trustees."

"Oh," he hesitated. Instinctively, a short tide of reservation swept from him. He looked at her askance.

"Facial recognition," she continued. And then, as if to rectify the non sequitur, "He . . . it's his company. We bought out most of the trustees' shares just the other week, I think." She smiled tightly. "But enough about that. It's all irrelevant. What about you? How are you." She touched his forearm.

"I'm well," he said. "I was living in Munich until a few years ago, but aside from the cold, not much to report." He shrugged. Here she was, in the flesh, and all he wanted was for her to disappear again. At least then, she could be contained within the faint whims of his psyche.

"You look good," she said, suddenly, and stood, looking around. "Would you like to get a drink? I've been dying for a moscato." The thin "s" left her lips flat, slightly parted. "*Moscato*," he murmured, a half-conscious correction that left the heavy consonant dropping like a shush.

She turned to look at him. "Yes," she said. "Do you still remember?"

When they fucked again, it was with a desperation he had not imagined her capable of possessing. Afterward, lying in the lily-white sheets, she murmured, with her back to him, "You haven't changed at all."

He turned to kiss her. "More than you think." They did not touch anymore. He lay flat on his back, arms behind his head, exhausted from her endless exertion. "It is you who hasn't changed."

But she did not hear him; by now her breathing had quieted to somnambulant sighs. He turned off the light, and away from her.

Bloom (editor's note: *the uncollected years*)

"You see," the difficult conversation would begin, "I am actually a flower." Not that she'd ever have the opportunity to broach the question. It would be many years, and several dimensions before she realized the myriad of ironies which accompanied her during her nomadic months in Europe. Few know of this period in !'s life, wherein she had followed, first a boy, then, a book, and finally, a clinging sense of desperate ennui from the Amalfi Coast to Cote d'Azur, to Nordic Tundra, and back again. The things which followed her: a worn copy of *I LOVE DICK*, a craving for intimacy, the unknown diagnosis and subsequent exile—these were trials she faced in paradoxical isolation, the incidents themselves transforming into pestilential epicenters of her life while terrain and movement seemed to vanish before her feet. In particular, it was on the stage of fucking that she waged her revolution, or, more precisely, revolution was waged upon her, and her corpse enlisted as half-conscious foot soldier. So it made sense, that these months abroad signified little in the grand scheme of !'s comprehensions, and that she took care to conceal their true events from the sweeping eye of the few interested in her life.

Maximum pleasure—was that what she was after? Or, pursuit of power—reverie, desire, respect (for wasn't even the rudest desire an admission of need, and therefore, vulnerability?)—which could only be afforded on the stage of fucking (consummation being, she realized, slightly less dismissible than the care afforded by fleeing attraction). But, oh, now that it's all over, we see that she wouldn't realize the impact of her naïf submissions until it was far too late.

The first pulse came in Milan. She had ignored it, in favor of denial paved by repression. But by the time she reached Vienna, the virus had flowered into an uncontrollable stem of poison so potent that she could do nothing but resign herself to the gynecologist and florist, in that order. The doctor didn't know what it was, only, they whispered to her behind musty doors, that she was not the first. The garden, it seemed, was the best-kept secret in all of Europe; a second spring that folded within the cotton lining of her moist jeans. Now that the seed had been sowed and the first bloom undoubtedly on its way, there was nothing they could do save confinement, daily watering, and a diet of antiviral pills which both she and they knew would do little to snip the bud. Perhaps it was an oversight on part of her caregivers: the sight of the dipping bud, gazing from her cavern, was a precious sight indeed—to snip it clean off was a violence unthinkable. What would the girl be, in the aftermath of this theft? So she submitted herself, once more, to the cotton expanse of the bed and the army of probing fingers until one clear morning, she felt the first pangs of pain in her lower abdomen and a pillow of dirt beneath her head. Hurry, she called to the nurse, it's on its way. When the team of botanists wheeled her out of the operating room, her face had been replaced with lilting petals of a venomous red, which spilled out of her mouth until their soft skin covered eyebrow to chin. Her gentle heaves emitted no sign of pain, but, in the absence of face, we cannot be certain that the operation was without failure (slight mishap, it is said, is known to have been common amongst these mid-century botanical experiments). A violet stain unfurled the spot of the pubis, and it, too, quivered with every sigh. At the edge of perception, by a corner of the bed frame, a single vine curled from beneath the blanket and wrapped itself around her toe. This was how they'd identify her—Girl With Vine On Toe, specimen 378—when the time came for burial.

They laid her in the soil on a Tuesday, beneath clouds that wavered on the edge of dissolution. At first, her foot wouldn't fit into the pot-sized hole they'd dug. Oh, dear, she'd thought, that hurts. By the time her lower body was fitted into the plot, however, she had grown tolerant of the stinging sensation that marked neural attachment to the host. When they were done, only her bare torso was visible, above a shadow of a bush at the opening of her legs. She leaned back against the brick wall and stared serenely at the planters, slivers of pupil visible from behind the curtain of petal. In place of tongue, she now had a long, snaking stem, so that she could no longer talk, but could taste the atmosphere and the tone of the conversation around her. Disappointment bordering on bitterness, one smacked; relief that tasted like the mild-sweet of honeydew, another. Every day, the procedure continued: daily watering, a dash of fertilizer around her waist, inspection by the botanist, then the surgeon, and finally, the Feeding. The team of scientists set up a camera at the base of her plot. Day in and day out, they monitored her measurements. She could no longer feel the cold nor gaze upon her as she used to; only, when it came time for her daily medication, she sensed a writhing start from the base of her pubis that ended in a ringing at the top of her head. Her body, as if it possessed a volition of its own, would begin turning and twisting, until her arms thrashed with the same elegance as the stem that rose from her lips. The botanists took note; the surgeons, with their thickly gloved hands, patted the clump of dirt lining the point of contact between her hip and soil, finding that she had settled so completely that no arbitrary division now existed. It was then that they stopped the antiviral treatments, and allowed venom-red petals to bloom without interruption.

On the hundred and fifth day, she woke from a dream and saw the sky for the first time that she could remember. A tickle sounded in the back of her throat, and, she found, to her surprise, that when she mimicked the gesture of coughing, a deep rattle sounded in the back of her throat. By the hundred and tenth day, her sound box had been rudimentarily restored, and simple phrases had returned to her vocabulary. The venom-red which had previously occupied the full terrain of her mouth now receded, and she found that, on good days, she could momentarily will its retraction. "Where am I," she muttered. Or, "I want to go home." But when prodded about the precise location of "home," she found that she could not remember, or didn't know, or was perhaps purposefully evading the question on behalf of her guarded subconscious, who knew then, as in the remainder of her life, that complete evacuation of normality would ensue at the sight of discovery. It was as if the id hoped, when no other part of her could, that some semblance of normalcy could still exist after the ordeal. But what normalcy was, it no longer knew.

She was discharged on the hundred and fiftieth day. Discharged, for that was what the surgeons insisted on calling it, but the botanists preferred deracination, a term which they repeated slowly to her until she could form her swollen lips around the syllables, and too proclaimed it with a jubilance she had almost forgotten. They knew little about the disease, but from the samples they had taken, they told her this much: she was a viral carrier of a lethal concoction, which meant that she was, firstly, contagious, secondly, subject to sporadic periods of blossoming, and thirdly, strapped to the antiviral medication for the rest of her life. The flower remained, though they clipped its edges. Former subjects, a nurse had whispered to her, had been subject to the complete decapitation of their buds. But they found that, once castrated, they lost, too, the function of their voice, having been left only with a wilting stem in lieu of epiglottis and tongue. They swore her to secrecy, but, as we know, that was hardly necessary. when she left the site of the clinic, it appeared, on the surface, as if she had never entered it. Trace evidence remained: for the rest of her life, she was obliged to inform the few partners she took of her condition, and postmortem interviews revealed that, during moments of peak emotional volatility, a red glow would rise from the back of her neck into the space above her crown, establishing the visage of a halo, or a blood-like taint, or a pair of devil's horns. She was never straightforward about revelations of her condition, preferring instead to open her mouth and will the bloom. "Unfortunately," she would say, "I am actually a flower, viral at that." For this reason, among others, she remained a mostly solitary figure for most of her life, a fact her less-informed biographers attributed to her intense occupation with the liminal, or her drug use, or general acerbity for which she became known, in the intimate society that failed to attend to her. Why we take interest in her today is a fact beyond me, but, this condition, known colloquially as *toxicum genetrix*, is now successfully immunized.

YEAR OF THE PIG
(colorized video, may 20xx)

THIS PROGRAM contains disturbing imagery and sound. Viewer discretion is advised.

KEY WORDS: slaughter, year, year of, eat, P, mukbang, muck, comfort, slurp, flesh

Act 1: Craving (Slick; Porous)

Act 2: Carnal (Slimy)

Act 3: Carnage (Smooth)

Sensations: plush, slimy, chewy (tender & hard), webbed Cyborg voice

I [Craving (Slick; Porous)]

Mukbang video begins to play, trails off after 30 seconds— replaced by the sound of rain.

It is 2:00 a.m. and I am feeling a little antiseptic. Oh dear … I've been thinking about feet. Earlier today, strolling down Swinney Road, a little arrogantly, bouncing on the plush lining on the bottom of my soles, I thought about feet. So rhythmically inclined I almost forgot the wet market. Oh dear. Clutching a battered copy of *Animal Farm* with my

elbow, I spotted the bouquet of clobbered trotters. Hanging haphazardly, as if in mid-jaunt . . . Oh, so many varieties I momentarily lost my breath, caught between webs of cartilage, flapping skin, and the angular thickness of their shores. Somewhere between a cut and a tear, it made me feel . . . I lost my step and Orwell flew out of my crook and into a smarting pile of dung, crouched on the corner of the bend.

Pause.

Oh dear, forgive me. I have scarcely introduced myself. My name is P, and I am about to die.

Chuckles bitterly.

Don't give up until the very, definitive end, my mother used to say. She'd snort a little with laughter, never forgetting that somehow, in the midst of it all, there lived an inarticulable absurdity, and perhaps it was only by confounding this absurdity that salvation could be made. Not found. The only thing you can find is dog shit, or else lose your paw in the effort of regaining your step.

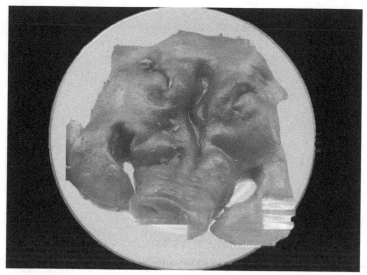

Stumbling on unsteady gelatin. So I did the only thing I could, I went home and washed, slathered a mud mask on my quivering nose. Then I slithered onto the couch and turned to the best thing I could find. I felt as if I might cry.

Video begins to sound.

I have awakened to the chiaroscuro moon. Troubled by a dream, I slide into the slippery cool of wakefulness. The light of the dim sky shines through the curtains like a drawbridge made of shadow. From my position on the bed I am covered by a thin sheen of smooth grey, which shivers and threatens to give way to the dispersed light cast by the extraterrestrial beast. Selene, they called her once, did you know? Selene. The word slips out my lips like a slip of fabric, muzzling my throat. Do you wonder what I dream?

Zoom out from the open mouth. Image duplicates, until screen is dotted by small holes. The holes shimmer, and the tiny videos rewind and fast forward. Fifty small hot dogs leave and enter small holes. Trypophobia maximizes.

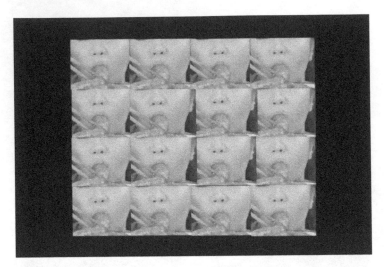

I slip a finger into the corridor of light and shadow now cutting clearly across my bedspread. I find that I can't move any further. And the air takes on a viscous quality, (*sounds of chortled breathing*) breathing like dreaming, or drinking, or any of the other hundred varieties of drowning. Feels like I am tethered to my bed, my limbs tied together. Funny, feels like I can no longer move, but am floating nonetheless, like a buoyant weight with no fear of return and none of departure. My arms are bound to my sides, and I can feel the coarse cord of leather cutting past silver microhairs, into the flesh. Do you know? This bondage is a sense of safety. The light moves through me, the shadow intermingles with my blood. The secret liquid inside of me simmers. I am possessed by a need to expel the abscesses that are arising in me, even in this moment. And when the abscess explodes—O! How beautiful it will be to swim through to fetid freedom.

Freeze on the motion of a hot dog.

It wasn't long ago that I fell sick. Rare kind of flu; I don't want to talk about it. But I am possessed by a colony of small viruses, this I must say—say, lest they fester with

unabated vivacity. Day in and day out, they multiply on the multispecies ecosystem of my body, contorting through my blood stream, cartwheeling through the marsh of my cartilage, seeping in the gasps I make between labored exhales. The abscess of this infestation grows ever larger, with no sign of explosion, and I am only left with a souring pain. I don't want to talk about it, but O! What have I done to deserve this filth?

Rewind action—food coming out of mouth. Continue for several scenes, then abrupt pause, and fade to black.

Sound of heavy footsteps ambling from carpet to tile. The clatter of what could be ceramic. Sustained sounds of vomit.

II [Carnal (Slimy)]

Do feel better now, won't you.

Clip begins. Simultaneously, projector begins displaying food on the tables. Amputated limbs in the shape of genitalia. Beautiful women with their eyes cut out. A pig's carcass.

So many ways to eat and so many ways to puke. Do you see those men and women, day in and day out, stuffing their faces with thoughts of pleasure and pleasure, only. At what cost? No, it's not violence I talk about, but the cleanliness of their *soul*.

I must confess to you something. Now, I must confess. Look to your neighbor on the left. Close your eyes. I am right next to you.

I am not real at all. In fact, I am the process and the process is me—I am an idea, never intended to be put into practice. But oh, somewhere along the line, the concept became the thing itself. Transformed by people just like you. Yes, transforming just like you. You think you can protect yourself by looking, but oh, my dear playthings, enjoy the visual splendor. See the plump dumpling, the marinated pickles, sending a stream of pleasure. Oh, you moan. You think you can look, but let me tell you, the thing looks back. You think you can survive the distance of looking but let me tell you. It bites back. Say "cheese." *Sound of a camera click.*

Look at these mouths. See how the abscess grows in and on them, see how the abscess spreads through and from their pores. There is a virus, and it is infecting all who breathe its musky scent. There is no evil, but there is a growing pit, marshy, gluey. It runs through my body and all I want is to watch these beautiful girls cavort in its fetid pus. I want to watch them eat me alive, and then I want to cut them open. Finally, let the dirt seep through, let its viscous underpass connect the prey with the preyed upon.

I must confess, I haven't been completely honest with you. I have been dreaming of fresh cuts. Oh, yes. Fresh cuts and squeezes. I have been thinking about licking my lips, so far up that they reach my mud-splattered nose. Oh.

Don't look at me like that. I told you, I am sick.

Oh, but I am hungry.

III [Carnage (Smooth)]

Darkness. Silence.

Can I tell you a little secret?

I can't get this sensation out of my throat. Once, a long time ago, I had the misfortune of stumbling upon a half-eaten container of takeout. Spicy eggplant, there was, and marinated pork. Oh, how I wanted that marinated pork. I had not eaten for days, and the sight of the browned fat sent rings of shivers up my spine. Upon closer inspection, a faint but fetid smell rose from the rim of the plasticware, but I was so starved that I barely registered the smell. I peeled back the cover and dug in, mouth first. Oh, but could I explain the anticipation that surged out of my mouth.

Only.

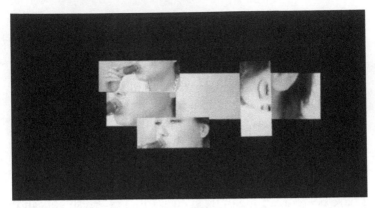

If only.

No sooner than the soft fat hit the roof of my mouth that I realized—something else had entered too. How should I put it? A swarm enveloped my tongue, and quickly trickled down my throat. It was as if the pork had been alive and broken into a million living pieces, which were now wriggling into every crevice in my fetid mouth.

Were it that I could spit out the bite, but in my eagerness, I smashed the morsel against my tongue; so split second, that the secondary sensation came as a delay, beyond reprieve.

I coughed, and clutched my throat, trying desperately to hack out the foreign intrusion, but it was too late. The harder I coughed, the faster the elements squirmed. As if they were a guerilla force on the move. By now they had expanded past the grand entrance of my throat, and I could feel them in the crevice between my teeth, wedged against the nubs of my palate, penetrating deep into my firm gums with their microscopic feet.

Oh.

Four screens alight. Hot dog eating scene fast forward/backward in repetition.

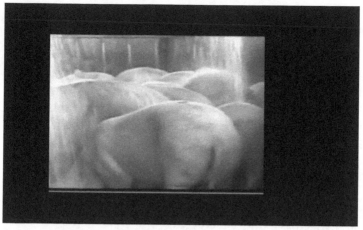

No sooner than I had registered their colonies in my mouth could I feel them in my stomach, swarming in clumps, torqued against my surprised organ, which began to churn. Something within them must have reacted against the acid within me, for I felt a rush of liquid, and a violent spurt of acid shot up my throat, bringing with it the crumbs of how many tiny corpses.

Yes, I am sorry to tell you this.

Video stops, suddenly.

You see, I have been sick ever since.

Even now, they live within me, and wake me in the dark of night. Clawing against my once-firm walls until flesh begins to grow red and pulpy from lapsed resistance. *Coughs violently.*

If the walls of my cavern collapse, what will seep, crawl, slither, out? I have dreamt this question for many years. I have not been clean for so long.

My time is near, and the swift knife awaits me. I have no regrets. Having dreamt the clobbered trotters, I know where I'm headed. Down another throat, where I will lie simmering.

Faster, with urgency. I want a good death. I want a clean death. When the butcher slaughters a pig, the first thing he does is bleed the carcass. Bleeding is a process of purification. It is only when the butcher bleeds the pig that he may prevent bacterial growth in the carcass, so that the flesh may be preserved. Pale pink, I will be. Can you see it? The smooth, pale pink of recently cleaned flesh. Sweet like lips whet with desire.

Clean me, before you eat me, will you? Scrape me clean and watch as I am scraped clean.

Whisper. Eat me, will you? Eat me and let me finally be at rest.

Mukbang video begins to play, once again. Pixelated, the image slows, flashes, and stops, until BLACKOUT.

Image Credit: Spirited Away, Dir. Hayao Miyazaki (2001)

diary entry (editor's note: undated)

sometimes, even through the haze of nicotine, she despaired. of what was a great writer made? some assemblage of coherence, poetry (which was nothing if not coherence, married to grace, wedged between chaos and the interminable pregnancy of rupture), nerve. writing it down did not salvage the situation: life, the situation, an endless track on which they wrote to pass the time. that is to say, the obligations of "urgency" and "passion" and the frivolity of "meditation." *what an endless exercise in ritualized performance*, she thought. but what did it matter that she thought—the words could hardly form in her mind. she had become distant from the language, so many variances there were, yet so bland, effused with empty gestures of vigor in her droll practice. on most days, it felt a puzzle from which she had tired.

she had not written anything of value in months, though the very idea that value could be attributed to something so abstract as the inventions of solipsism made her tired. could she write anything to irrupt the corrugated steel before the eventuality of their return, which is to say, could she write anything to set fire to herniated disk and bring the relief of cold? lately, she was always cold. she could not feel comfortable no matter which way she lied. it used to be that the heated words would flow out of her, so filled to the broil was she, with things unsaid, heretofore unthought, and (so she thought) worth the pretension of utterance, to a room empty with holograms. she felt differently now. almost like a mouse, she felt, walking in the streets with her heart thumping like a broken wheel, scared of what was to come, scared of what could have been, unable to look at the transparent archive of the sky.

it could have been her shoulder. for months, she could not rid herself of an uneven aching, which sagged her left arm and gave her the loping appearance of a body in pain. she was not in pain. the ache throbbed to remind her of an immovable pin on her side, drawing toward the ground, holding her firm in discontent with nothing to complain about. now, no matter which way she laid, she could not rid herself of the pricks. no matter which way she sat, she would not bring pen to paper, for fear of the stiffening effect such an action would inspire. what happens to the mind during the stasis of a stiffened limb? her thoughts ran laps around the faded watercolor of the racetrack. everything fainted to impression, and she rubbed her shoulder blade, cut by the jutting bone, glued to marinated flesh. there was nothing to say, no, she would not be the one to say it, disabused of her position between the subaltern and her inscrutable wavelengths. hello, are you there? henlo, ar yU thar? xoxo, fi-yer in the cuh-vuhn.

it occurred to her to seek out the source of the pain. as a means of unpinning herself from the unfair advantage of gravity, to which she had already succumbed, but---. soon as she touched it, the ache would disappear, pastel imprints ungraspable by thickened fingers. her body lacked the grammar of pain; rather, it lacked the basic structures of language acquisition necessary for such sophisticated interpretations. chomsky, deleuze, derrida, and their scraps lay splintered between the cake of the neck and the scapula's knife. it was as all things she had attempted to fix: the solution remained burrowed, becoming so vague to the naked eye that she was brought to question their reality in the first place. but this was all cliché, in so many words. that was the problem. there was no longer anything to say, only ways to say it, and she, artful deceit though she may be, could see no more reason to respect the embers of the craft.

in germany, she stayed in the home of a mixed-race couple. D and L, they were called, and they had an adorable two-year-old whom they referred to as eloise, caramel-bun, and peach. the young family lived in a three-bedroom apartment on the outskirts of munich. though it had been seven years since they arrived, the house felt unevenly worn, its wood-lined walls croaking in baroque contrast to the newly refurbished guestroom, whose glass chandelier sparkled under fluorescent light. the only drawback of these accommodations was their distance from city proper, so immense was the length of the road that ! felt keenly its weight every morning as she set out to falsify the living of her life. perhaps suburban isolation was cause for the home's disjunctive erosion, she thought one day as she made her way slowly to the bus stop. after all, didn't she, too, once live in dizzying proximity to the simultaneity of shab and sparkle? what good had it done, except to make her notoriously bad at leaving places.

the bus stop bordered an empty expanse of grassland, whose negative space served as constant warning and puzzle to her. she could imagine being murdered here—not her, perhaps, but the body of a doltish blonde girl, easily occupied by the dark haired inscrutability of her captor, lying amidst the fraying strands. she could feel the clumps of dirt beneath her palm; a tingle set off by contact between back and packed ground. fifty meters down the road, a cemetery peeped from behind a cluster of trees, the tops of greying tombs drawing subtle distinction from softly swaying foliage. who could be buried here, in such permanent proximity to peace, after the mangled screams died out.

D was notoriously wrapped up by her faith. that the bodies of christ could sustain a woman without stripping her of the qualities of goodness which led her to the holy triumvirate in the first place was a fact foreign to !. D was a sweet girl, whose innocent reprieve and simple spirituality complemented exactly those qualities that ! lacked. conversation between them was gentle, marked by an assurance of care that allowed both to be, in turn, calm and playful, so that their exuberance retained a meditative quality. ! did not know herself to be capable of such untroubled amity, a welcome departure from her usual tristesse, which marked the pitiful relic of the christian church she had long left.

spongy light greeted her when she emerged from the warm darkness of the subway. as if to mark her entrance into the vivacity of Life: a cinematographic affair. but she never quite managed to roll beyond the opening credits, for, once she slipped on her sunglasses and oriented herself (heavy denim, leather heels, a tousle of grey-blonde bangs), she found that, in fact, she was alone. engrossed clusters of passersby (school children? frivolous couples? she could not tell) strolled down the street, bumping into her at intervals just sporadic enough to keep her from calm. like a strip of disfigured tape, she stuttered, jumping back at every touch in approximation of a hiccup. caught in this high-strung loop, she felt as if she could collapse, giving way until empty canvas sank into the ground, and she, a spurt of dust settling into heaving textile. an approximation of an approximation of a border between parched skin and cutting wind.

lately, she had begun to question the chokehold of the slim. that morning, she had failed to fit into her choker (a vine-gold affair that always threatened to catch in her hair), but succeeded in stuffing herself into a pair of low-cut jeans she had long thought to have outgrown. the body was strange in that way. still, a nagging anxiety clawed at the edges of her eyes. for years, she had orbited carefully within reach of the "acceptably plump," occasionally sinking to the emaciated, but always quickly rising again to the mild, and, with more time, simply plump. *what did it matter to be skinny anyway*, she thought. there was a time in her childhood when the smell of a book, or the coagulant of paint could draw her out of herself entirely, until she was block or paper or crayola unhesitant. a transcendent absorption, the likes of which she only dreamt about now. when did such fluidity disappear, and flesh cast itself as prison, confining her body to the realm of the claustrophobic, that propositional longing in the tune of could have, or should have, or that most dreaded, perhaps. perhaps, she would scribble, followed by several vague mentions of a Thinker, in lieu of an idea. the world of the known felt immense and distant from her current station, a narrow platform on which she had only space to pace. *when had she lost the resolve to move?* she thought fondly of those days, when, aching to get out of her body, she buried it (raw, without the extra effort of marinade) in the texts of ahmed, keeling, weil, merleau-ponty, extracting bone and marrow in lieu of her scraggly mane.

in attempt to find the ancient kernel of herself, she would lose her body within the sauce, inadvertently achieving that which she had set out to do all along. academic rigor, her professors beamed condescendingly, or, you're the most talented literature student we have, their voices dripping with the foreshadow of rejection. or, you're trying much too hard; there are unspeakable heights over which you've yet to scale, so we look at you as dust sculptures, should you one day harden yourself thus. she longed for the effect of knowledge, that reassuring solipsism through which the mind abandoned platform for ballroom and sent ideas on foxtrots tracing themselves and each other, becoming endlessly self-referential, analogic to the brink of deconstruction—all with a flick of her eyes. such translucent reverie, whose self-referential knowledge exceeded narcissistic dictate to open up exclamation for true inspiration: a clarity of sight emboldened by possibilities' clearing. cartographic ignorance: she remains unknowing of the to-be, only sure of the impending syntheses ground by the organizing principles of Touch, Style, and Form.

there was nothing skinny about the dialogic laboratory, all utility and smooth operation as it were. was it a desire for the dissatisfactions of exteriority that drove her back to the surface of her body so that she could wonder, self-consciously and then scathingly, if her lipstick was still intact, whether her calves were flattened beyond the point of flattery by her too-tight jeans? what if yoko ono was onto something: it is not the Body which needs modification, but the game into which we have entered It? that is to say, what if the Body were not here to stay, and transcendence were possible given the collective effort of rewiring? rewriting? if everybody in the world gathered at 14:00 eastern standard time and thought, sincerely, "I Am More Than A Body," would the second coming descend from the sky? or would we find ourselves more trapped than ever, in a universal sunken place from where only neoconservative insistence can emerge, disguised as complaint? sometimes being skinny meant suffering a dissociation of equal discomfort. never mind: she had not ventured farther than the edge of the platform in a long time. now she was afraid that, with every gust of wind, she might blow away—or, in the absence of that, she would remain heavily unchanged, moored on the dock of her desperate immobility.

sometimes, she wished for a physical manifestation of the ontological invisibility from which she knew she suffered. wouldn't it be easier, she reasoned to her cramped mind, if one could refrain from being coated by another's gaze? wouldn't inscrutability be nicer, or even its most extreme iteration, an incomprehensibility which elides the boundaries of literal perception, and its deeper parallel, figuration? invisibility, or selective presentation, or a lonely girl phenomenology aborted of hips and breasts and the soft fat of stomach: lonely girl phenomenology in a scopophilic vacuum. too often, she wished to lose sight of herself. lose/site—she was sick of this body, sick of its inevitable surrender to existence and nonexistence: it remained a bifurcated street, a pathology, when all she wanted was to fly.

Note from the editor: i suppose all this is for naught, since, following !'s exit, we have yet to hear back reflections of the post-matter. how at peace she must be, that i cannot help but think this is the way she would have wanted it: a wisp of denim, the glimmer of a smile, her profile always just out of reach. how we preserve our loves, that reveals something of their Essence: a fundamentality liberated from the inconsequentialities of epistemology. "when form is in place, everything in it can be pure feeling." finally, she had become flattened to the precise point of her most flattering profile, laid out for facades of impartial evaluation, sentimental regret, nostalgic longing. all reactions to death are variations on the singular theme of desire, honed, to be in jest over some specific dimension of the deceased spirit.

american symphony

andante furioso

speculative fiction, or lies i tell my uber drivers

speculative fiction, as told to uber drivers, may be the truest form of the memoir there is. S sits herself on the operating table, splayed out sans serif daggers and frankensteinian sentences. in pursuit of a lost limb, i follow. toward an affect of belonging: something blue, something borrowed, the melancholic retrieval of broken dreams, and the confessional novel, or how not to leave oneself raw in the chemist's tube.

sex and the city, a novelette: i listen to terry gross's well-meaning cut on the radio, in a yellow taxi covered by soot. ninety minutes of recrudescent racism featuring cultural translators who've accumulated enough social capital and intellectual gentility to be consumed by the middlebrow white audience. levittown, usa: what an honor to have become an entree in the bourgeois literary diet!

we drive over the town green and i switch one body for the other, ripping through skin like mantle through wind. everywhere, white ladies come out to greet me. i am their idol, or else i am a cheap symbol of their possible redemption. this would not be a problem, except that i hate the word priapic: an adjectival derivative of the minor greek god Priapus, guardian of the garden and beholder of giant dick. the god of small things holds a priapic hoe. the god of small things spills forth from her cramped domicile holding a carrot, held by the too-tight strings of her apron. the carrot cake hair of hausfrau, out of the house and frowning. HOW CAN YOU RUN IN SHOES LIKE THAT. they are always glancing at me, with faces like banana bread muffins and wonder bread with flour sprinkles, floating away on geriatric shoes. reluctant senators of the NPR constituency.

sex and the city, a novelette: not enough space to explain to my newfound friend. whose cheek folds like apple crisp. i look down at my fishnets and become ten again: CAN A CHUBBY GIRL EVER BE PRETTY? i look down at bones in search of a home and become a ten again: lose the fat, lose a limb. wandering bones read like a priapic curse, stamping stretch marks with the vigor of stilettos.

speculative fiction as told to uber drivers read like unresolved desires peering over the edge of ego death. solipsistic psychoanalysis always turns unaffordable: like, suddenly, you find yourself with a boyfriend and a hundred thousand dollars in debt. a feeling like you've lost the mesh between skin and flesh, and everything is friction waiting to be punctured. where did the time go? suddenly, there are no lies any more.

to die for a dream is to escape so wholly into the phantasmagoria of another world. to be in transit is to die for the dream, and to catch up with the living. to die for a dream is also to die in that dream: to divest all in the pursuit, and in divesting, to "have" a body again. to "have" a body as in: i lost my body wanting, and now the body that exists is not to be "had." a sentient body no longer strapped to ethical convictions and reservations about the love story. a body that can finally care for itself within its solipsistic orbit. ISN'T BEING WELL ALL WE'VE EVER WANTED, MOTHER?

castrative fear is all that i got: a penis, a limb. pursed lips as thin as lead, husbandry operated by the plowed. i believe that there is no god. that, furthermore, in the ashy dawn of crematory bliss susan sontag can still be referred to as a writer. i am still a writer, but if the dead could cohere. a writer who has stopped to write, to bury herself.

gluttony at tanforan

I.

the tanforan mall, home to hooters of san bruno, hollister (of the west coast), dirty glass walls, concrete jungle, kiddie jungle. and, perhaps most importantly, that ironic triumvirate: the star-spangled banner, the growling motto of the west, and their brethren, the bare flagpole. the irony of the "american" flag framing the court of the tanforan "mall" is palpable: not least because the tanforan, before its concrete makeover, was a racetrack and the northern california japanese internment center. yellow men, yellow beasts. anarchy framed by the mellow sky. you can still see the traces of barbed wire, only now there grows a stubby line of hydrangea bushes.

the "american" flag: who is american? the tanforan "mall": who decided to curse the poor horses with such an ugly home? where was america, anyway. i think the concrete offers a step toward better times.

the only person who hates the mall more than me is my father, who hates the idea of me at a mall enough to murder a small horse. not that a horse has anything to do with my being at a mall, but if you shoehorn me into the right retail center, i just might buy one. i've always wanted a nice mare. i certainly spend enough time with them at night.

my father's calculus of debt methodically includes me as an expenditure. but the eliding boundaries of the "nuclear family" threatens to leave me out of his reach, and both of us confused. too, my father is plagued by (including, but not limited to): narcissistic subjective dissolution, a gendered horizon of responsibility, and a fixation on the patriarch(y) of the tang "family," which is to say, he is, in fact, an investment banker. call us the provincial chinese branch of Merill Lynch. i am dr. tang: stroke neurologist, part-time psychologist, and a phd from the university of tokyo.

but no matter what i do, my feminine failing renders any panacea to my father's ailments an impossibility. medical miracles are doomed trivialities in the periphery of tang concern. comprised of books, makeup, and the vain misgivings of the everyday, the cure to melancholia is not, contrary to the doctor's orders, a healthy dose of sertraline and a daily routine. the vain misgivings of the everyday happen also to be everything i give a shit about. dr. tang, in her entirety, is a feminine misgiving of the everyday. her sins: depression, anxiety, bulimia—all viral forms of home and love "sickness." her frivolities: of painted nails, expensive sunglasses, and the occasional glass of merlot. deadly enough to kill. her life, with its fragile edges and poor substitute for curatorship, is simply not worth enough to sustain her daily routine.

i wonder. what would gabriel garcía márquez say about the pathologization of my gendered failing? love sickness is not a punch to the gut. love/sickness is in the time of cholera. the former is a meningitis of the heart; the latter an aphrodisiac.

never has a matriarch of the tang "family" surfaced. rare was it that a woman—who was not, and could much less imagine herself as, a constitutive strand of the implicitly professed tang fabric—would willingly bear the weight of several generations of man-children. tarantula sized tantrums require a professional extinguisher, and the tang fold can produce only bug swatters.

things no one talks about in the field:

[redacted; it's not talked about for a reason]

we are the fray of the "family," or, the anxiety of a ranch owner in a cattle pen without a corral. who is a tang? who will calculate the debts owed and oversee their uneasy settlement? the concrete steps of our country villa seem like a good place to start.

methodically built and angular in structure: stairs. polluted only by the kelp of emotion and the cacophony of overlapping voices, which render explosive the torrent of facts disappeared. like the occasional smattering of chicken shit which accompanies the cascade of secrets. one learns to walk around the fecundity. others learn to sweep.

the last time i went to the tang home i became struck by a violent cold. expelled lumps of coal-sized pus. not very polite dinner conversation, i'm afraid. that i was a mere mortal, subject to sickness despite my american upbringing, did not answer any of my cousins' questions about our fundamental differences. ontic differences, they might ask. maybe we are made from different stuff. they and the neighbors wanted to know every parameter of my life, but they are careful to establish boundaries for themselves—things they know i could not know. things they could not, but would, tell me.

II.

DO YOU THINK I WOULD MAKE A GOOD TROPHY WIFE?

i do, he answers before i can change my mind. i'm disappointed. even joanne the scammer knows: it's all one big circle jerk of misogyny. the artist as art object is rather: the woman as art object. occupant of the curatorship of her life, to each her own caucasian home. so to speak.

here's a reminder to polish up on adrian piper: the personal and the theoretical as Praxis and praxis.

once a dude tried to hit on me in philz by pointing to my "got privilege?" sticker. do you know where that's from, he asked me. curatorship, challenged. the artist's theoretical knowledge: loopholed. i gaped at him. i do not say he was aroused by me. to hit: diminish, degrade.

to be feminized as an artist is to be simone de beauvoir as a manic pixie dream girl—sartre's, but with a sinister underbelly of her own. the artist's impeccable taste: a chiaroscuro, and in this case, a delightful proclivity for underaged girls. sex, seduction, a room of one's own. these are the trappings of the modern woman: artist in her self-actualized exceptionalism.

i hate that phrase, self-actualization. other words i hate: priapic, wanderlust, escape, adios (for its misuse as a flippant adieu), bildungsroman, self-discovery. i knew a white boy from our recruitment camp at stanford who took a year off before yale: to go bicycling in turkey. finding his middle of the road destiny in the middle of the East. it sounds like an indie movie, i told my friend. "riveting"; "human truth"; "touching; a masterpiece imbued by ---'s charm"; rollingstone, new york times, some white yuppie from the new yorker who thinks he can write. one big circle jerk of male navel-gazing. to be masculinized as an artist is to be heroic, a mastermind, and graced with inherent knowledge of the Bigger Purpose. which for him inevitably includes crazy sex, a sizable inheritance (or accidental trust fund from his estranged grandfather's long island estate), and a peculiar but situationally justified taste for the absurd. white boys are always so basic: either they actually trust the ethnic restaurant's yelp reviews, or they really just don't want to try anything new but are afraid to say it. everything else (connoisseurs, pimps, hoarders— and the brick that hold them up) is fake.

the off-color trophy wife fits in this schema as a flavorful chapter that veers toward the salacious. there is space for her limited humanity as neither artist nor woman, but artist woman: the well-oiled harmonica of an abandoned cinematographic feature, starring none other than the turkish bicycle and its sunburned rider. she is the only audience of this budgeted art nouveau. as she sits in the empty cinema, sipping on a gin and tonic, she wonders: could narcissism be read as simple masochism? maybe it's best not to be seen.

III.

that afternoon she sat barefaced in dolores park, musing about that particular brand of abrasiveness she had come to associate with her tar-tainted secondary education. that same bitter aftertaste which, aroused by reinitiated mediatization, she tried immediately to repress once more. she had done this many times since her uneventful departure from an altogether provincial childhood. with it, she left: suburbia, sagacious heads (cursed by baldness), and, less successfully, a grudging admiration for whiteness which bloomed from initial infatuation. but weren't all childhoods provincial? the thought of vanilla nauseates her: the creamy deception of it all. no, it was better to stay away from ice cream, and all those plaster-variances which became too easily tainted or, just as randomly, threatened to swallow you with their infinite blankness. she had forgotten the particularities of her befuddled adolescence. the return of its coldness left her numbed in surprise.

which was better: to be cared for in acts, or to be regulated in the taxonomy of friendship as a self-sufficient being; a potential competitor, in nothing if not that persistent departure from a testosterone-induced haze of self-worth. she didn't know. or, she did: no one knew. it was impossible to know. she had realized, in conversation with friends torturously made and discarded, that care cannot exist in a state of isolation. it was always getting left behind by the simulacrum of her life: this, she decided, was the problem. she could only ever near a semblance of care—peek the rosy horizon of (that mythical essence!) love—before she, that is to say the "i" of her fleshy cast, decided to impose its unforgiving will on the metaphysical court of her life's narrative. so that she remained constantly on the verge of reunion with the rumored landmark of care, only to be disassembled, time after time, in the name of the love story.

the abrasive recurrence of her childhood friends—those peculiar specters from a previous life! whose cotton candy induced coma on the neoliberal merry-go-round she would otherwise find distasteful. but their silent presence made sense in the pothole-riddled paradox she identified as "living." what was it to live if to do so is to enact a constant delay of living? the transient space between the actionable term (and a fossilization of the thing itself) and the phenomenological extension of its "being" initiated by continued occurrence. the only assured thing, she thought, was that of her drifting, which, at the moment, felt worryingly directionless. she felt libation at the prospect of tunnel vision, only, unlike joan didion, she could not yet drive. the high-way was indefinitely unavailable to her. so she worried, simultaneously buoyed by her anxiety and driven directionless because of it.

IV.

I MIGHT HAVE MUTED YOU ON FACEBOOK, all her lovers said this.

shuttled along from one pothole premise to the next. she ran after herself; her "i"—the self, split within the matrix of the Holy Trinity—alternately played catch up; twisted.

the game of life, which proved to be a combination of catching up and leaving herself behind as a perverted souvenir. IF ONLY THAT WERE GOOD ENOUGH TO BE TRUE. scampering after the Good Life. she wondered how long it had been since she inadvertently muted her self. it must have been the last pothole-cum-vacuum out of which she had recently emerged, skin papyrus pruned and hair coarse. into which she was uncertainly plunging once more; she had only traced a shadow of the actual escape.

he looked at me with those big, lazy eyes and i knew it was over. we have been a part of the event of the end for a long time, pet.

V.

i shared with him the same improvised sublingual connection i enjoyed with my dog. it was irrationally rare, despite its simplicity: invention of agreed-upon symbols/ sounds to act as a signifier, the resurrection of form, and voilà, linguistic invention. the dog/human connection: i scribbled frantically.

significance
history
linguistic relation
emotive symbology
reframing "friendship" "family" "ownership" between womxn + Dog

the latter was a terraced thought of two parts: a consideration for the commodification of dogness that was an extension of basic capitalist critique. the second was a doubling back on the teleology of consumption, which included questions of functionality, value, and the death of art.

it was at this point that she realized his doe-sized eyes shared with Dog and a new character, J Did, the same performance of exceptionalism.

J Did, it may be said, has perfected a tone and thus cannonized herself at the cost of reducing the THING to less than "it"self via nomination. the moment "it" became a tone (cannonized, generic), her writing—its pulsing, ontic core—died.

J Did is the dissipating drop of estrogen in a vat of cis-driving testosterone. your evil man-brother's favorite informant (whose bruised crush he does not reciprocate). this was what she realized, as she picked a stray slice of grass from the canvass of her cellulite. but by then the sun had faded and her things, she realized, had blown halfway up the hill from her.

gospel of failure

on most days during the monsoon it is hard for me to leave my bed. five feet from a view of the city: marvelous. whispers of sub rosa quivering: oh, what possibility! to be found under the blankets, a solipsism so quiet it can almost be ignored. to stay is to demonstrate loyalty of the highest order—to thyself, temple of flesh, to sit through the collapse and touch the jagged remnants. failed apocalypse: did you know the strength of your own walls? no, you say. i wake up, lurch. swimming organs can't drown; nevertheless, you teach me how to breathe.

how loyalty can squeeze itself to ten and thirteen feet but still never touch the ground. clench, goes the bed frame, but it's your diaphragm that swells with the effort of breath. nowhere do i feel the weight of metal, having resisted the urge to return "home"; crawl into bed, stare at the ceiling and windows unaffordable. i remain loyal to the cause: some sort of catharsis; sated convalescence. that is the commitment i have made on paper, a solipsism so quiet it almost feels safe. to be: elsewhere, far enough to betray the sob, its grip. this is why we fling sobriety; out, out, out dirtied panes chased by dust and stifled moths. i think about how it feels under the covers, always better than here. relax: not (t)here. too relaxed and the temple empties itself; desecration, and you have been banned. alien, save the curve of the thoracic spine, but what a waste; away; dismay. green bodies swallowed by the pills of the cotton; think back to travel across the sea; sink in sea; drown in sweat; swallow the stinging salt. today i awoke loyal only to the bed. turn against the spring, muffle under the must. the bed as place: of cathexis; the barge, a green-glass prison. children will be born of the night, draped across the posts of neuropathy around which sea-drenched teeth cannot curve. cauchemar kids, who swear allegiance not even to their creator. cauchemar kids, who bah on command and do not sink. four-legged kids and a stomach so smooth, lined with only the finest wool. how the walls sway as they climb up the hill.

we speak the same language, you say, but i only heard saltwater gargle. i have finally floated, but my head is beneath the water, and you teach me to breathe but my blood, too thick too heavy to lift, floods the spine and drowns the cave of the esophagus. my gasp the syncopated rattle above symphonic bah's. how strong are your walls: do they bend? what writing stains?

i have come to the conclusion, lying on this swing, that lies are the only answer. lies holier than denial, more potent than sacrilege. lies: the only movement of agentic assertion, or objecthood made luminescent. lies as those which lay the temple's final step. above which the stiletto wall sings.

bereave

my life is NOT: toward an aesthetics of depression;
the orientation of feminized confessionals ("diaristic").
it is

a bowed head held between one's hands . . . it is "my
god, my god" . . . (in lowercase, of course, because
there is no god)

> *what do i believe in? the private life*
> *antagonizing culture*[1]
> mediocrity, melodrama, in unequal measures
> a scatological dig: a broad city

interminable mourning for myself

what does it mean if—a scaffold upon which we hang
the tailcoat of our desires, what does it mean if a
scaffold upon which we hung the rear cut of the id?
got irrationally angry when the barista delivered my
lox bagel to the wrong customer. what does it mean—
slow, burning anger native to bourgeois mediocrity
(in another tongue: repressed monotony). one day my
daughter will write of me:

> *she made me aware of how she eludes all*
> *"theoretical" efforts to grasp her logically, to reach*
> *a knowledge of her. she revealed a fluidity, a will to*
> *elude as persistent and as shrewd as other peoples'*
> *frankness and self-revelations.*

is a rimbaudian innocence a tango with the absurd? it is
a method of evasion? the fluidity of partial evacuation:
a pendulum between tangled positionalities, so what
is natural is an interest in symbols and systems of
signification. the best poetry is constant play with the

ludic entanglement of partially evacuated positionalities. the best poetry is an elusion and illusion, and june, who inspires the feeling of anticipation: constant readiness for the marvelous, an avant-garde collage and surrealist orientation of touch—but. on the scaffold of tango solipsism, the original postmodern project, already evacuated, empties its corpse once again.

is it possible for performative text to overtake the Real (a teleologically scattered position in relation to the mediated "r"eal)? is the body one without the text?

she lives without pattern, without continuity. as soon as one seeks to coordinate june, she is lost.[2]

what do I value? the coordinates of loss. the incomprehensible, inconsistent logical system.

"self" preservation rooted in desire not to give (away), but to possess and "reside" in deracinated poststructural "sub"ject-ivities under a negotiated discursive freedom. isn't that the purpose of elusion, aided by topographical inconsistency, uncertainty? rimbaudian "innocence" that is also tactical brilliance. irigaray, on the coordinates of loss.

[1] editor's note: Susan Sontag, *Reborn: Journals and Notebooks, 1947-1963*, pp. 5-6

[2] editor's note: *Diary of Anaïs Nin, Vol. 1*, p. 30

bear-reave

i hate the phrase NO PROMISES, NO EXPECTATIONS. it is, in and of itself, a perverse expectation; a twisted promise. freedom in name but without any of its trappings. NO PROMISES: an idealistic longing for freedom. NO EXPECTATIONS: delusional appeal to freedom which results in final displacement—death of postmodern womanhood. freedom in delusion, freedom in manifestation: a perverse logic.

in 1931, anaïs nin finds herself as a third member of the torpid couple that is henry miller and his then-wife, june. the word couple, from the latinate *copula*, means something like connection or tie. as part of this knot, anaïs nin seeks no promise nor expectation—she understands june and henry are notorious for their capricious appetites. henry is demanding and jealous, but june is the picture of good: even in the absence of promises and foreseeable reciprocation, she possesses an undeniable allure, which is to say she is a perfect picture of feminine vulnerability. june is like an open flower; when assaulted by the wind, she offers no resistance. one has no choice but to weep for her, and then sweep her up in kisses.

> *EVIL IS AS LIFE AS WELL AS GOOD. i want to live without idealism and without ethics. but i am not free. i am incapable of destruction.*[2]

june destroys reality; her lies are not lies. they are roles she wants to live out; she has made greater efforts than any of us to live out her illusions. june is displaced from a Real but bound by narrative trapping in a textual real. if you wish hard enough, the actor becomes the script; the author manifests her text into a living, breathing void through which she rediscovers her fleshly body (mummified, floating). but what about the subconscious is there to romanticize? desire, shameful hedonism.

to say that freedom is Aestheticism is a gross reduction of freedom's possibilities and the infinitude of the free. "beauty for beauty's sake" is inane, naive, and the worst kind of lie (incidentally, the type of lie i most often tell): a misnomer. to hell with reason, wholesomeness, artificial unity! long live the cartographical impossibility of the haunted assemblage. i cheer for the coordinates of loss to the syncopation of the peanut gallery's chant: NO PROMISES, NO EXPECTATIONS.

if signification is fossilization, my obsession with symbolic inconsistencies and incomplete logical systems is an attempt at movement from the death drive of the lingual archive.

> you want to force delicate, profound, vague, obscure, mysterious, voluptuous sensations into something you can seize and violate. but will you caricature it? why do you want such clarity from me? . . . i never understood proust's need to know, to be present almost, when albertine was loving someone else.[3]

you cannot possess without loving. is the linguistic drive a gesture of perverted love? if sex and birth are essential possession, i want ontological possession, which is to say i want to be sure of myself. to be myself. but i just AM. june just IS. a body: no longer tethered by significatory clarity. inconsistency is a freedom of its own.

nowhere in the law of metaphysics does it say that resistance and acceptance are natural antagonisms. it is possible to refuse something and accept it. the only possibility of self-possession lies in becoming the language, whereupon there are no more expectations or promises, or the oppressive consistency of the copula.

a connection is no longer a tie; the same thing which at one moment sustained you becomes nothing at all in the next. time is the only constant. freedom—destruction—an end to discursive limitations on desire. this is what i do not want, i think. i spin from one subjective commitment to another. sometimes, what i just WANT is a staggered victorian in the berkeley hills and a four-year-old girl. do not listen to me: i have nothing worthwhile to say.

[2] editor's note: Diary of Anaïs Nin, Vol 1, pp. 42
[3] editor's note: ibid, p. 55

mark 10:9

she could not imagine being another person and loving herself. HOW'S MY DRIVING? call (503) 287-5966. she took a snap. lana del rey still called and she could not ignore the crooning, so she saved the number for another time. when justice needed to be restored, she would hearken the scattered pictures: of phone numbers and spare body parts, and query. what is the worth of customer opinion? she wondered this as she perused. static rippling across the cruelty of the cityscape, music to watch boys to.

the embarcadero reeked of burning steel, by which i mean the money of new construction. which is also to say piss and rotting vegetables. it became grimy stitches that sew together incongruous felicity, the sterile and the decomposing, so many bodies in proximity so as to create an echo of the architectural collage. colored by a general shadow of rot, the city makes mediated suicide, plaid and ashy corduroy, a plausible fiction.

i scheduled a date to the munch exhibit with P, but so far she has kept me waiting just shy of an hour. uncouth, but i expected little else. not sure why i am even here in the first place, since i made it clear that i only valued her as an easy fuck. emphasis on easy. minimal interest in the coarser details of her personality, desires, personal history. priapic autobiographies have distorted all of my lovers: rather awful of me—i should end the reciprocated violence. but what do i value? the private life. to speak instead of talk, so that even flaccid smiles—of P, of A, of G, the countless before and the savanna after—can become the front of delusion. i'd want daughters someday, P tells me above the botanical garden. she flicks her wrist to grin at me, yellowed scrawl stretching from navel to the elbow's tender belly.

fictions i tell my uber driver: yes, i am american. other small lies. lingua franca cum lingua violence via the futility of engagement. do you know the tower of babel? bible-thumping as verb. we all spoke the same tongue once, he said, as he held the scalpel. inhale, the anesthetic fog. SMART, BEAUTIFUL WOMEN SHOULD PROCREATE, the doctor tells me, so make sure you get started early. her hand grazes the edge of the table as she authorizes my certificate of eligibility. A COUPLE MONTHS, A COUPLE YEARS. tales from an impending mirage, between the crossed and the faded lies a love spread over palimpsest. finally, narrative différance: a well let not her put asunder. together, let us sing a hymn. sometimes she spins herself into a discursive bubble and then loses sight of it all. a prick, they call her, but i know that it will never exist as beautifully as it did in her head. impossible realities: they bury her, the small wound.

doloroso

the important things go unsaid, like, i went to the piercing shop to get my cartilage piercings looked at, then they took my infected jewelry out of my pus-encrusted ear. the whole time i was thinking "good riddance," shivering horribly while my piercer cooed nonsense like, "oh, that was in your body" as if he were miming cunnilingus, very medically vague at that. i suppose the masochistic desire for fleshly puncture is not so different from the carnal desire for orificial penetration.

whenever i say the word penetration, i think about my ex-best-friend krista. we used to have a joke about penetration, but i don't tell it anymore because it makes me too sad. basically the premise was that we understood implicitly the violence of heterosexual sex, both of us being straight-coded semi-gay girls. the premise was also that we understood the catch-22 of being hypersexualized east asian femmes trying to, you know, rock it. reclaim it or something. i forget.

i got my infected piercings done with krista in st. marks, at a piercing shop called "elite." it was more cube than shop, but it was much nicer than any of the other ones on the street, so we, with our bourgeois sensibilities, had no other choice. in retrospect i would have said to my nineteen-year-old self, never trust cubicle chic. and, do not aspire to be a member of the ruling class. but i didn't know what i do now, which is that my friendship with krista was much like the to-be-infected piercings. a bad trip that turns progressively worse. i think, now, that the piercings were the beginning of the end.

after he took out my blood-rusted jewelry, my piercer scraped the inside of my ear with a gauze pad and applied dabs of medicinal gel. i could feel something oozing in my ear, but i was afraid of asking too many questions. those piercers know what they're doing, and they don't like it when you try to assert yourself. krista was always very good at asserting herself while pretending that she wasn't, but i was always the more verbally abrasive one. it was very easy to play good cop/bad cop that way. a slap on the wrist, in goes the needle. almost painless. but now i was by myself; there was no needle going in, only dubiously rusted gold coming out. i pinched my forefinger, but it did nothing to stop the pain. krista had asserted her way out of my life, leaving only a bad exit wound behind.

i saved the jewelry, even though my piercer told me not to. i remember thinking, what a waste my twenties are.

—

danny and i sit on the narrow strip of sand, splayed blankets a colorful juxtaposition against crumbling rock. to wrap the entropic in cloth. i arch backwards, feel the breeze sigh against my glistening forehead. all is but sun and sea, and brine, slapping me on the ass.

recently danny has gotten it in his head that we are to be instagram famous. sure, i tell him, why not? i have always wanted to be a model. i think everyone our age wants to be a model, he responds. a jagged slice of rock breaks through the shadow of his hair. we talk about skinny gaga, how weird has become the new cool, that queer is now the new crew. gaga has dropped the a. her glitter now gags. when everyone has on a wig, hair becomes obsolete. there is no longer anything to cover.

i used to be skinny. in fact, ask my mother. she is always slyly checking the circumference of my upper arm. gauging how much meat hangs from the needle we call bone. meat—tender, caramelized by the sun. you've lost some weight again, she notices on our walk. oh? i say, feigning surprise. we have had this contention for years, now, ever since i hit peak bottom of one hundred pounds. at five foot eight, i stood like a slender pine. the wind whistled through my hair, threatened to escape through the crevices of my spine. my mother was once a pine, and even now she worries about the direction of the wind. she has not been one hundred pounds since she became pregnant with me.

it has been almost ten years since the release of the fame monster, danny and i realize. when do icons die? or is their immortalization only consummated through ossification? i feel like fun is reserved only for the famous, danny tells me. the only way to know anyone or do anything is to be somebody. kylie jenner's catch-22: the only way to live in los angeles is to be somebody. the only way to be somebody is to live.

danny tells me all this as he snaps pictures of me. i practice lounging, imagining a sun-kissed mausoleum. under the effigy of once-crustal cliff, i arch my back in approximation of down dog. channel my inner guru, my most important teacher. namaste, forget the corpse of the ground. exhale.

—

i was trying to be less !. this manifested in: excising ! from my textual declarations. lowering my voice in speech. being constantly conscious of volume in speech. excising squealing from my vocabulary. adopting a white sonic aesthetic. look at me, i can use words like barthes, pinot grigio, shibboleth, žižek, etc. too bright, off-white.

do you know why i failed? damned ! in perpetuity, to the glee of men like james lambast. a word weaver, he fancies himself. sits in the arm of sinecurism, spends time refuting charges of racism. ardent defender of neoliberal anti-identity politics. we are all the same but cannot sing kumbaya. the book of anonymity is dead. he never had a song. james lambast and his wife karina discovered me at dinner with a prestigious literary prize winner–blah, blah, blah. who had slicked back hair, form-fitting suit. a trim kind of masculine, with a seamless vocabulary to match. proclaimed leftish, though unarticulated. silent during the white man's war of anti-identity proclamation, made me want to curl up in a closet, to escape his calculating . . . torso (racialized, indeed).

james lambast discovered me in the slicked back lobby of his founder's groin. karina had drilled stubbornly after the drops "revolution," "teleological obscurity," and "coloniality of power" flowed from my lips. big, fat droplets. dewey from exertion. a dewiness potato james and sprout-wannabe karina open their mouths toward; pine for, unknowing.

i wish i'd spit on him. you still want to cackle, james. stammering away in your crumpled trench coat. does it please you to know, we will never exist as possessives to you? !. we are not derivatives of an already dying twig. when you lie awake at night, james, bothered by an unscratchable itch just beyond the horizon of your scrotum, know the prickling sensation for what it is. a curse on your   !

—

the hammer is the most unimpressive museum i have ever been to. it is a gnat on the face of all other museums–scratch. it is like all other museums, so, a giant larva pod glittering with the performance of progressive bloom. an infelicitous consummation of capital and self-righteousness. political utility dissipates with faltering language. like: the John V. Tunney Bridge curves into an installation piece that is simply: end White suPremacy. black print against red fluorescent base, 2008, artist, poor bloke who believes he can change the world with Art. or die trying. to subvert the wealth of the ruling class by selling his tears. you tell them, but you're screaming into a literal tree. so guess what, boy: John V. Tunney doesn't care about your statement piece. his bridge bends its back to slap you.

that's the problem with white aesthetics such as that which clutters the breach of the hammer. without real stakes (in the dome of the vault gallery; roundabout of the guggenheim; the grecian facade of the getty), they comprise a self-consuming game of pretend. two women coddle a sobbing toddler at the mouth of the John V. Tunney Bridge. why do people bring babies to museums, unless to reaffirm the museum's inherently useless quality? a place so purposeless even babies–the most potent of us–fail to grasp any semblance of potential.

in the dome of the hammer's main gallery payne and tanaami have cluttered a suite with drawings of japanese monsters feeding rocket ships up their butts. something something approximation of japanese arcade game visuality. looks like obsession with anal penetration, to me. directionality, desire, consumption. of who? mass culture does not care to be abstracted into such sterile forms. missiles are penile whether they are pixelated or not. payne wishes to penetrate—tanaami, octo-limbed schoolgirl, the orient—so desperately, that the marble floors of the gallery are littered with the ash of his desire. tanaami splays androgynous agents across reams of silky paper. someone should go watch some hentai already.

the hammer doesn't know what it wants or what it is. its carcass sits like a glorified playpen in the ash of the city. the color must be right, the installation perfectly arranged, but can we cut the shit? who has time for oversized adult toys when the city is burning? you don't have to sell "water is life" to me as if a cup of beer. public sex requires only a condom and consenting parties. don't hold it in a mausoleum. isn't it all a game of make-believe, anyway?

—

did you know. a young condoleezza rice used to live across the hall from benjamin netanyahu's parents. ?. contempt breeds contempt. D tells me i have an encyclopedic knowledge of Facts No One Gives A Shit About. correction, i tell him: Known Facts One Gives A Shit About. for example: at the time of buddy holly's death (plane crash, tender age of 22), his wife (of six months) had been pregnant with their first child. she miscarried. Known Facts One Wishes To Give A Shit About: good things do not everyday happen to good people.

sometimes my mother speaks to me from the future, and i feel the scalpel cutting me out of her womb. when i move to san francisco, i will have to take care of two dogs. empty the trash. slide across wooden floors by myself. familiarize the wind. mist. crayon-marked walls anew. when she leaves, i will have to lock the door. when we leave, the carcass of the grass will shudder in relief. can a mausoleum be alive? when you leave, but no, you never really leave. it's only a matter of when, but not how. when i leave the effigy of the monument stands, and all we have to show for it is eternal ignorance. does amnesia amount to immortality? forged in the dew of stale saliva. orgasmic light be damned.

HOW THEY WILL REMEMBER HER, or, AN EFFIGY FOR ETERNAL PIXELS

- she loved to talk loudly, had an abnormally large forehead, and an asymmetrical jawline. that's all i really knew about her.
- brilliant, but could never get a clue. you know what they say, you learn some, you miss others... and she was always weighed down by the absence of the others.
- thoughtful, interesting to talk to. woman of integrity. nubile body, mostly funny. (but i'm lying.

she was, most importantly, servile in the best way.)

- i wished for her to join me. i have yet to return her voice, pay her the deposit. she was always on loan, you see.
- she was vain, spoiled, oft depressed, and had a predilection for tantrums. but i loved her simply for the fact that she was mine. her narcissism only made her more in my likeness.
- i wish she had lived to love me under the aurora borealis. when i see her next, i will remind her of the knife she left in my drawer. my bruise the size of a fetal kiss.

did you know, my best friend connie once told me. that the chemical compounds of ash take on the molecular structure of an X. really: i imagined a hundred thousand X's scattered across an urn, quadriceps so fine they threatened to cohere. HERE LIES XXXXXX XXX. XXXXXX, XXXXXX, XXXXXXXX, XXXXXX. Known Facts One Gives A Shit About: the dead don't really haunt us. it is we who haunt them.

when two sets of lips cohere, an X is formed. she signs the letter: till death do we part. what X has joined together, let X put asunder. can a mausoleum be alive? if so, let X run her heart out, away from her own spindly limbs. let the wind blow her into the sky, until she is ash no more, but sand. cohering on nothing but bare flesh, sliced open by sweet fetal kisses.

—

to make a thing into a thing is to labor into being through channels of the sublime: a constant readiness. a permanent pregnancy; motherhood, widowhood, anticipatory equalization.

birth, from the norse: burðr. to bear the becoming of a thing into a child is not to tolerate its transcendence, nor to midline its existence. the birth of a child from your pen is a thing done unto you. all you do is whisper. not your average bear, breath hot, heavy. the only growl that comes from the monstress.

for several days now my lower abdomen has pulsated with complaints of the surreal. it is a pulsing so absurd that i can spend hours curled on the futon. sharp shoulders like a hyena's laugh: the absurdity lives! in fact, she has only gotten lighter. when the shivering comes, i will knock my head into the edge of the coffee table. mahogany's revenge, you will think to yourself, but i am slippery, like a dog without its fur. you cannot grab me anymore. the only scowl is that of a bear's, readying itself into action.

the doctors will have nothing to say about the spasms. they will jab my tongue with metal sticks coated with elastomers. you grimace at the sight of plastic: so puerile. how can a child bear it?

then, eyelids heavy. i have to do some writing, you tell your friend. so maybe this delay, it's a good thing. a call to get busy, in otherwise creative and intellectual ways. we are not your average bears, but i have already forgotten what i meant to say. droop.

my yoga teacher, the goddamned angel, directs me into a spinal twist. drop the hips, and into a pelvic opener. the hips are where tensions are held: a phone buzzes. sometimes for years on end. she says yoga is the meditative act of letting go. to unite body with soul.

buttery flesh crisps at the thought of reunion, to turn a fire into joints.

to bear the thought of holding on to power, i stop giving blow jobs. you ask your friend why she thinks blow jobs are, what was that word, empowering? um, subservience can be reclaimed. hugh hefner is a dirty man, but he can't buy the blow job. she says, i've already insured it for a million. cosmopolitan dot com lost in a narrow bidding war, but i bore it out, and now poor hugh can suck his own dick.

A SNAPCHAT. two hands cup her tender breasts. they rest there for several days, undisturbed save the red nail polish.

the night after the incident of the spasm, i dreamt that guanyin pusa slept next to me. i'm tilted, they told me. i draw my eyes with magic marker. christine? i ask, but they only touched my forehead and disappeared. i worry i might have sworn in the name of Jesus Christ one time too many, and then the shudders return.

there is little talking required during the act. but i have always been a talker, and clearly you can't bear it. all i see are the soft waves of your hair. periodically, you sniff. two lines of blow, and i can't do the job anymore. guanyin pusa has left me, and my boobs, that god-given gift, droop in recognition of their velocity. suddenly, i want to leave. stop trying: milk will not turn to honey and all buzzes will end, after all. what we are is never murmured, but the arousal of the speech act has always depended on its causal enactment. no, thank you. we knew, from the beginning, if the beginning could be so borne. we have been a part of the end for a long time, baby, and that is the last thing i say to you.

—

. . . imagine my surprise when the door opened to a doleful brown woman and a little boy several shades lighter. a moment of disidentificatory confusion and—ah, it all made sense now, susie and her husband, the very pale mr. everystein. in all manners of extra, the everysteins had not only a townhouse in san francisco's choicest district, but—susie everystein's personal assistant whispered over the phone—a penthouse in the four seasons facing union square. hoisted high above hoi polloi, their wealth boasted the unapologetic eye of demure condescension: extolling american history for toddlers, a picture book of venice, and a belief in their own effortless superiority as sure-footed as the satin sheets which lined their four-year-old's bed.

but children were all the same, and he clung to his mother with the immediacy of a shrunken shadow.

in the dawn of my regret, i had fallen for a boy three months younger and several tax brackets higher than me. at what was to be the end of our short-lived affair, he invited me for a weekend on his parents' ranch in santa barbara. fed up with my dewy-eyed indecision, my mother—no doubt sniffing the lingering putridity of an overripe peach—warned me not to go. the look that susan everystein gave me—doe-eyed, limber, hooded with the rust of acquired command—inspired confusion that called to mind the wave of regret which lined my aching throat for months after the fact. the sting of her tinkling laugh, and an eagerness unbefitting the yardstick of her performative wealth brought me to the doorstep of my ex-lover's guesthouse. where she was white in everything but appearance, he wore a swarthiness often mistaken for some exotic derivative. you are---, her glossy mouth puckered uncomfortably around the foreign consonants of my name. carefully perturbed by her ability to pronounce it, an unwelcome reminder of our similarity.

the brevity of her graciousness bit like his hand; stung like the morning after; her immediate exit rang the silence of his shame. she turned quickly, and i thought how it was only after the decay of the rotten peach that i could bring myself to remember the way he shifted his body away from mine when the stable hand caught us kissing over breakfast. hired help, meet---.

night fell, and susie's four-year-old, in true fashion of the nouveau riche (being bred to withhold the pretense of a young lord), woke crying. only when i held him in my arms, his plump legs intertwined around my torso, would he fall unwillingly back to slumber. susie and her draconian husband returned to the young lord sprawled across me on the couch. his light touch befitting the kiss of a butterfly; i wondered how many more senseless girls would be called to serve. in pleasure and in shame.

—

somnambulant pulses. i did not dream of you.

> At first I took her as being exceedingly proper, but
> I soon realized that she was simply executing the
> language. She went word by word. Every letter had a
> border. I watched her wide, full mouth sweep through
> her sentences like a figure touring a dark house,
> flipping on spots and banks of perfectly drawn light.
> The sensuality, in certain rigors.[1]

contention contortion convention cabaret. the rapport
lives on interest, borders dancing around the words.
converse contort cavort ca . . . cadaver. sometimes my
mother speaks to me from the future and i can feel the
scalpel slicing me out of her womb, tongue delicious
singing of praise–beauty in sharpness, sensuality in
exactitude. i wonder if you read this still.

> It was, she cried silently, enough to suffer as a woman,
> an individual, on one's own account, without having
> to suffer for the race as well. It was a brutality, and
> undeserved.[2]

to miss amiss remiss miss chinatown san francisco. missed
wave missed wave missed gait mist grate. she who wears
the crown atop ivory skin. i have not eaten chips in two
years. on my own account. to suffer for the race as well. we
too possess scalloped cheek folded eye limber stomach
and ache ache ache for upturned nose. turnip nose.

yesterday, en route to yoga class, i thought of a name for
my dog. the dog that owns me. paid two grand to have
me delivered, caesarian style, out my mother's womb.
two grand for a scalpel; dance to the death, in certain
rigor. the dog that owns me named herself lourdes, but
i thought: oh my. my. my. that will not do. the umbilical
cord, my.

your dad is different, my mom says to me. i do not have the heart to tell her: the umbilical cord, my. the womb, your. my mother smacks her lips. i knew when i met him, that man is unhappy. how must we talk of addiction if not, unless, through pathology? the sick body, rested on the laurels of her chest. postpartum, happy. happy. happy. that will not do.

i think i am addicted: somnambulant sighs, the curve of the spine. aching ovaries. how can longing hurt so, if indeed it is happiness (my) toward which i turn. if indeed it is happiness (yours) toward which i fold. somnambulant sonatas are the only caves in which i can hide. might we dance, i ask you. teach me. my, the umbilical cord, father is different. box step, bontemp, three two one twirl and a one one one one one one one one one one. & fin, to fold body sick in motion, stick on floor. what is she doing now? the sagittarius moon taught me how to waltz, and mid-step we let go of that which weighed us down. the sick body, in flight—

som som som somersault soar soon. the hiss of the air ne'er lose you, forlorn. look to the right, and look to the left—

[1] editor's note: Chang-Rae Lee, *Native Speaker*, p. 4

[2] editor's note: Nella Larsen, *Passing*, p. 225

lucentezza
graziosa

reason for the season

when i was finally permitted to see my mother, moments after her surgery, she turned me away and asked for my father. his presence centered her in a way that mine did not, and in that moment i realized that i was merely a sublease within the emotional contract that bound them together.

my biggest fear is that my mother gave birth to me out of a sense of duty: the way she had done most things that determined the tempo and arc of her life. or maybe: i was something she had insisted into being and later regretted, so full of ancient vileness am i that i drove away even my mother, the one from whose flesh i emerged, who grew me inside of her own body. you are going to be the death of me, she says to me sometimes, when she is angry. just like your father promised. i cry and stamp my feet, scream *panic attack!* and *fuck you!* and *you make me want to kill myself!* over low-resolution video. suddenly i am eight again and everything my mother says makes a perverse logic i can't escape. somehow she knows my every nick and groove, so versed is she in my infantile reasoning that perfectly rehearsed memories, under her scrutiny, become riddled with the cracks of doubt. i want to make "scorpio finagle" a commonly used moniker or more sonically pleasing phrase. everything my mother manages becomes infused with a driving essence of her, until it no longer knows self or can distinguish between life and narrative written by her.

in this way my mother is the original author: the first artist i knew. but if there is one thing that defines the making of an artist and the subsequent phenomena that extend from her cosmic birth, it is solipsism, and solipsism cannot stand when one is confused by two, and i can no longer know self from the seed growing inside me. periodically i ask my mother why she is so scared of life. her answer never changes and we rehearse the same conversation. i never remember what she says but i always remember to revise my question from noun to adjective: timid, cautious, risk-averse. my mother is so functional it scares me. to see someone so apparently bereft of flesh capable of cruelty and cardamom in equal measures is to see a human, despite my doubts. it's strange when your mother becomes alive, or when her skin grows a consciousness of its own. when the waves move according to their own volition, the carefully projected solipsism between moon and self is broken, and the artist is in peril. i want to be the kind of competence that makes my mother scared, which is to say, how do you stop yourself from becoming something that you revile? what does a home without a home look like. when skin peels by its own volition and wounds remain unaffected by salt, who do i turn to for affirmation of my sanity? in a court without witnesses there can be no operable version of the truth. when did we give our voice in supplication and become unable to distinguish food from the hand that feeds? the mouth that speaks? the contract a narrative, debt driving the plot toward a wail: forsaken worlds sting like future exhausted by rehearsal. i have forgotten my mother's answer but we rehearse the same conversation until—i sit trembling before the ghosts of my fetal whispers. the same conversation: it is not her life, she, of which she is scared, but its opposite, which is to say, its derivative: the birth canal, the death drive, me.

dear S,

i wonder how we will part ways. it haunts me, this curiosity. what will be the last thing you say to me? my final glance—of regret, gladness, uncertainty? i know these things don't really matter—blasé as they are—but i keep an emotional tab on my romantic ventures, those digitally curated phenomena. so i don't forget; can construct a system of valuation, nomination. either way. i wonder how it will be with you.

i read a *cosmopolitan* article about the "12 relationships every girl is glad she had." i'm a hack for these "girl power" "rah rah" facades. call me a retrograde, white-aspiring shadow of a planet—i am, as the shallow rack knows, guilty as charged. what isn't so easy to dismiss is sympathy. i'm so glad you're type number four: the one for whom "timing just wasn't right." of course, you and i know it wasn't just timing that was at stake, but i probably would have ended up either a "professional artist" (of the private island variety), or a socialite with a cocaine addiction. maybe, somewhere between: anywhere, with a tragic flaw. to think that for a moment, i rested on the terror of the abject, before you shredded me with sans serif daggers. the possibilities of positivism: two bodies weighing on each other.

this is the recurring mare i dream: you, the subject; i, the witness neighing from afar. it does not take a genius to know that gravity is the only element of our relationship that promises reciprocity. in my dream, you called my mother a yellow monkey. i woke up with mouth agape. my suspicion of your less than savory nature confirmed, internalized complexes unwrapped: motherhood, glass shards, dripping tongue. all this came rushing back when my mother asked me what "prime time" meant. of course, she was also the first and only person i called. how fortunate it is to flail against the current, always striving to turn the tide into some comprehensible stroke. some syncopated alphabet. i am against interpretation indeed—what luxury it must be to experience without the impetus of meaning-making (that stultifying effect meant to fossilize; monumentalize for the sake of desecration). what do i believe in? the ephemeral. the Real, without attachment.

what if, instead of depression, we just called it what it was. general feeling of listlessness; proclivity for casual sex; irresponsible behavior that inadvertently turns self-destructive; a plague of ennui; the symptom of negative fucks. fuck classification, categorization. my neurosis, like all neuroses, defies the charlatan's feeble fingering. unlike most lovers, it is loyal. you will never shake the intimacy we've built: sleepless nights (and blazing afternoons). i wonder if no more wondering. tragedy is not to be spun; loss is not to be caricatured and reli(e)ved. what a masochistic ritual. i still dream of her soft kisses, knowing full well the shallow tenderness they beheld was due for evaporation at any moment. still, i could not stop dripping. warm blood on burnt concrete: a trail up the i-10 coast. i had successfully deluded myself into a chekhovian melodrama with a happy ending. so, really, a grimmsian tale. i had finally succeeded in deluding myself into thinking: i deserve it all. but of course, i don't. the sentence of that narrative mold is romantic imprisonment: a duplicitous term that calls upon its victim to endure the pangs of empty desire, and then believe that vacuous longing to be worth writing about. to commemorate a vacuated mausoleum. to dance on the grave of a grave. can such deaths occur? can such living, postmortem, resurrect the spectral Real.

the more that i reference our body of text, the less likely my manifestation. i think the problem is that i am the book. how many artists speak only through marionettes of their work—metaphors of corpses, outcast, inlaid. what i mean is: the creation of this book is necessary for my living. which is to say, it is not quite "creation" that pens this book's existential impetus, but the fact of its adjacency: as an extension of the glacial Real. look at me, writing of an entity whose ontological abstraction—the abstraction of an abstraction—can yet be verified. this book is an act: of catching up to the Real. i used to say that i will not write, that the articulation of a coherent belief system is a desire for destruction. to live in the Real is to abandon the pretenses of its capture: the temptations of falsity (which is the written simulacrum). to live in the Real: to anxiously circle one's position against interpretation and its more innocuous cousin, signification.

but the Real is a series of events locked by dormant potential, so the artistic responsibility of experimentation is to resist dictation over the course of manifestation. to be open to—and anticipate—the impossible futures springing from the past. so to write as living: to mourn. to build a grave of a grave, and then lay to rest.

yours---

J did not

decades before the invention of "humblebrag," joan didion launched herself as the messiah of changing times. *"what we are witnessing here,"* she writes in her 1987 essay on doris lessing,

> *is a writer undergoing a profound and continuing cultural trauma, a woman of determinedly utopian and distinctly teleological bent assaulted at every turn by fresh evidence that the world is not exactly improving as promised. and, because such is the particular quality of her mind, she is compelled in the face of this evidence to look even more frenetically for the final cause, the unambiguous answer.*

heralding the lost tribe of white male anxiety across the early tide of social revisionism (and that dreaded promise of "milk and honey [for all]"), ms. didion maintains an impressive commitment to the seriousness of her craft. of course, it is no surprise that two decades after the disparaging review, doris lessing has won the nobel prize for literature, while ms. didion lives on, shrouded by the comforts of the upper west side, impervious to her cult following and dismembered list of accolades. there is no argument that her observations (meandering sentences graced with the accuracy of butchery) and poetic unwinding bespeak the skills of an artist at the height of her career. amidst the laborious birth of new criticism, ms. didion adopts the gestures of critical thinking and the shadow of intellectual freshness. but what begins as an anxious retracing of the profound quickly grows flat. in its place: a poorly disguised appeal to rationality, the age-old trick of traditionalism. like many critics, ms. didion is a woman of her time. within her discursive scaffold sits a criteria of artistic rigor still orbiting around the solipsism of Aestheticism and Impressionism. of those explosive moments promised by Surrealism and Modernism, there is little trace: the crux of her criticism lies in the claim of artistic purity. social problems, those pedantic sites of practice toward which lessing is so drawn, to didion appears as distraction. no longer an "artistic problem," lessing's commitment to social realism, and her agonizing response to the failings of progressivism lights the final fear within the middlebrow structuralist's limited imagination.

what this fear is, we know not. but the fervency of its resistance chokes ms. didion's otherwise tactful gerunds. chiefly, one feels the nervous energy centered around her extended exhortation on the virtues of resignation. lessing's vision of social progress, her tortured tango with the spiraling teleology of revolution, we are told, is hopelessly naive. to look toward the future as a site of actualizable utopia; to even hope for the possibility (now assuredly destroyed) of a promised land (of the nondenominational, which is to say, socialist variety) is to shroud oneself in fictitious longing. we tell ourselves stories in order to live—wasn't it joan didion who wrote that? but the unspoken addendum, apparent here, is this: beware the sentences of the narrative prison.

ms. didion is at least partially right in her deterministic fixation on the present. revolution refuses cartography: to deny the appropriative powers of neoliberalism, the revolutionary ontology over which ms. lessing seems so concerned has no teleology. in many ways, the revolutionary drive is an orphaned affect—ms. lessing understood this and latched on to it the prosthetic of care, in the form of narrative. ironically, however, it is the trappings of narrative which frame ms. didion's aversion to such a project of (in)coherence. new criticism's boys' club, of which ms. didion was an early, gender-bending member, cavorts amongst itself to capture the authoritative voice of demise. too, its members sit smugly on the sidelines of disaster—structural inequality, racial violence, genocide of the poor—glibly issuing affirmations of their own foresight. of course it is easier to author social pessimism. joan didion and company are the original nihilists, vying to be narrators of the End of History. these kinds of writers, as ms. didion demonstrates, are the worst kind of messiahs. at least ms. lessing had the tact of uncertainty. the nihilistic refusal of her deconstructivist narrative by ms. didion is an evacuation that lacks imagination. new criticism, it seems, prefers the solipsism of its own self-righteousness. in it, the promise of impending demise is forgotten.

but i say fuck "truth" and artistic proclamations which believe, naively, in the moral orientation of the Real as stultified je ne sais quoi of the past. the scions of liberal america may shrug their shoulders, sip a martini, parade in the new literary language of ms. didion. observing, through her eyes, jimmy baldwin's disbelieving guffaw, they may actually believe in the implacability of their hallowed witness; she who is the last column of rationality amidst torpid upheaval. too bad ms. didion is no darling of baldwin nor of those dreamers whose stilted relationship to her articulated Real has become swallowed by casual impetuousness. what the dreamers know, but are afraid to say: didion's work only ever reflects, but always fails to near actualization. do not tell the gloated prose: "it sometimes seemed to him that for love to work it had to be fair, that he should only tell half the joke, and she the other half."[4]

i am tired of ms. didion's posturing: prophetic pessimism as a frontal defense against the unwinding reaches of the avant-garde. worse yet, she, as an emblematic figure of the straight-speaking midwife of white liberalism, is (mistakenly) embraced and consumed by the ruling class *as* the avant-garde. did we expect anything more from the disciplinarians of art, gatekeepers of the means of production, the coloniality of power? alas: systemic injustice allows no room for taste.

despite being political retrogrades of the worst variety (or, more likely, because of it), ms. didion positions herself as a voice box issuing traditionalist reassurances. by focusing on the futility of progress; by internalizing the peculiar discursive embodiment of apathy, ms. didion neatly wraps the "post"modern in vintage hermes and stuffs it in a velvet bag. all of this to say, the establishment survives on the foolhardy explanations of writers such as she to keep itself afloat. they have a financial interest in the canonization of ms. didion's eloquent narcissism. paradoxically, it is not nihilism or even apathy for which the ruling class looks toward ms. didion. rather, they seek for demise to be explained away—as an inevitability of the far distant, as a natural function of progressive impossibility; the a priori evils of man; what have you not—in effort to preserve the presentist bias of capital production. and so it is that, in truth, ms. didion pursues the currency of temporal lag. the declamation of naivete and utopianism serve as a facade above her deeper commitment to art as distraction. panem et circenses, now, for a post-apocalyptic era.

demise, explained (away) by the anti-matriarchal figure: the schema casts ms. didion as the madonna in reverse (or, just how the madonna was meant to be). together, they are the "true" third arm of the holy trinity, where the only whores are those sexually depressed, utopia-arching "liberated women" such as ms. lessing. but exhortation kills art and the sex drive in equal proportion. what didion does not realize is that within the formalism of the boys' club, she is the anti-midwife; the abortion doctor who has lost her scalpel and so can sit only in the musky wake of fetal collapse. it was jasper johns who said, sometime after the turbulence of the '70s, that artists are the most respected of the servant class. ms. didion would no doubt disagree, but as a witness with limited agentic gesture, her opinions matter not. despite a dry cartridge, the ink of bewildering change continues to flow. the proletariat's growing dissatisfaction, pushed ever forth toward the edge of the horizon, has already begun to seep into the folds of the Real. what a legacy ms. didion has left us! now, the task of art is as anesthesia: to divert demise into derision. the leakage of talk ensures that, for all its meandering, ms. lessing's writings will remain: writing.

[4] editor's note: Tao Lin, *Bed: stories*, pp. 15.

archie panjabi

it's politics—not i—that is too dramatic. framing my pentagonal room are a series of long rectangular windows, through which i watch the sunset from my bed. the sound of julianna margulies' voice and america's "last" "great" "drama," before i lose myself in the 24-hour news cycle. this is the last golden age of the great american sitcom, when retirement sanctions respectability, so emergency rooms and the sex—turn tepid from anticipation. sex and—the city is no more. i should like to move to chicago. retrace the steps of susan sontag, margulies of another era, several mediums displaced.

delicious words such as swallowing. and its synonyms. tempestuous siblings who i have lost among pluperfect tense and hendecasyllabic. how can you remember something you never knew? i wander the streets of berkeley remembering all the lives i have not yet lived. delicious words like spewing, my wisdom to the masses. for two hours every day the netizens of berkeley, california turn off their laptops and turn up the radio knob. crooning the color of verdant collage, so we can forget ourselves amongst the 24-hour days. one hundred twenty minutes minutes the sound of transition, day somersaulting to the next. melodic integrity and the steady cymbal, like the invention of the album and the disappearance of the radio personality. we love so much the canonization of personality. such as, the paternal figure of paternal figures: a simulacrum, the method of peddling through layers that borders on the reductive. the great american drama, last of its kind. the woman grown, girlhood expanded. how can i imagine womanhood when i have already lived my best years as a girl?

the great irony of sex *and the city* is that a show about the navigation and acquisition of male approval could be hijacked by four women, who manage to turn not only the plot, but the very substance of the sitcom, into a solipsistic universe of white femininity. this has been said before. what terrible humor the white woman can concoct. what deceitful tales she can tell.

sitcom is loosely defined as situational comedy which stands (or, more accurately, sits) for the pleasure of the test audience. hello, are you there? i was just wondering how much they paid you to sit through this shit. maybe you found it in the garbage and thought it well enough to reuse. maybe it appeared on your floor; utility turning, forget turning, beginning to orphan. maybe it never appeared at all and this is all solipsism turned sour: the kind of white-lady resignation carrie bradshaw and her fake friends forced for the camera in season six and movies one, two, and three. blandness, too, can have a sting, like battery acid eating into plastic. oh, maybe that's where you found it. an oozing that turns white to transparent, plastic to air, and you can almost make out the coils wrapped beneath rubbery film.

in *the good wife*, julianna margulies is served by the presence of archie panjabi (masturbatory dream of my girlhood in *bend it like beckham*). i see myself in archie's thigh-high boots and the crook of her eyebrow on which my aspirations hinge. like prosthetics the weight of a hair, you know. i should also like to serve julianna margulies, in the twenty-third hour, when i save the day with three inch heels and sardonic refusal. i am impressed by the way whiteness cloisters itself in this show, leaving enough room (always) for inclusion. but what if we don't want to be included? archie panjabi has disappeared, and the last great american drama, taking her cue, followed. there is nothing sacred, and very little good, so naturally whiteness follows the best thing it can find, even if it has to laugh off refusal and rub the sore spot where plastic heel dug into ruinous flesh. like i said, it is politics that is too dramatic. never the brown woman, whose body is never disappeared even as it is always evacuated. even her ghost is pilfered for fabric—julianna's next costume—so that she is responsible for everything, *everything*, even after she has died. the white woman of (white) women screams about the solipsism of the 'hood until the myth of subject coherence threatens to tear. so do i, but i had already abandoned the hood (the 'hood of the hood), only listened to smooth transitions and jay-z, whose genius is apparent in frank ocean. parent-hood, adult-hood, woman-hood, mother-hood, the sea breeze.

when i was eight my parents enrolled me in a seventh day adventist afterschool program. it was supposed to keep me busy with homework and snacks and playground time, but it came with free bible lessons and conversion therapy which they didn't know about. which they should have known about, because it was a seventh day adventist afterschool program. i met eve and steve for the first time in the red brick church at the corner of richmond and 39th. heard, with my very own ears, in a musky pew (pregnant with a kind of baroque possibility—a rich, maudlin red) of (st)eve's treachery, how they ruined their one chance at an everlasting, pre-transcendental peace. eden is a kind of delicate transparency that garbage bags maintain as sulfur dissolves polyethylene. from the rib of the dumpster, an infelicitous union, an impossible divorce. the white god's prefect represented by plastic—what beautiful deception he can concoct! what sexual tension his bolt exudes, flat and narrow like the pumpernickel expanse of carrie bradshaw's face. maybe that's where you found it. plastic draped like foreskin over cracked shell, now that's

some white lady bullshit.

i wonder if julianna margulies would like kanye west.
whatever, to smooth transitions and the minute hand of
the twenty-second hour. taylor and i might still have sex.
i made that bitch faaaamous. i made that bitch heinous.

k Now

there is a scene in this show i hate-watch (the title of the show is unimportant), wherein the love interest of the main character (a writer—white, pudgy, pale) accuses her of spinning tales that sound made up. "i don't make anything up!" the writer exclaims. we remember how, merely minutes before (in sepia-toned time), she had spitefully told her boss that "one day, i will write an essay about you in my book, without your name changed." we consider that this show (the brevity of whose title fails to match its televised duration) is the meta-fictional meditation of The Writer, a real person several dimensions displaced, who authors and stars in this very solipsistic (but, you will wonder to yourself, perversely indulgent) show. i would name this production: mundane spectacle, so easily it manages to naturalize whiteness and settle into an upper-middle-classed humor—of debauchery, dereliction, and delinquency. as befit the fabled children of this mythological country.

storied daughters and woven breasts, i make nothing up, only pull loose clench of yarn by way of caressing you. touching cheek and yanking your nose, fingers slipping hair matchstick rustle. dissolving you or—devouring you by sight. to pull you closer, like she fists loose-leaf: nothing made, up another paper crown ashy lips colored in one sepia-toned breath. everything so dark, so pitch black but—bright flash. next scene: sepia turns white skin to ultraviolet ray. like needle, so hard. porcelain without life, like this, exorcism a la luxury of self-invention, and, i don't make anything up, except the story of my life, so bright it touched your life. and yours. and yours and yours and yours and yours, and i don't make any of it up, i swear, just your life and yours. and yours and yours and yours. not even the story of my own life, so naturalized as self-mediating subject am i that i proffer my face, mush as foundation and the glacial cavity in my upper brow, to praises of beauty. so endless is my gape and the only refuge. sepia-toned children that stab your eyes out and spit in your skull. so endless that cavity, the only pause: way forward? no future. nothing more made up. no thing more real.

failed woodstock a la fifth grade picnic. in this no thing world there are no names, and there is Noname. DONT SMOKE TOO MUCH WEED, reads the alarm on my phone. stoned "i" am capable of fear and embittered responsibility, but god (and where may she be right now— tucked under my bra, behind the swollen fold of my cye) knows that nervous energy drives failure, preparation and well-meaning dictation—the stuff of missed opportunity.

two extra sets of quotations, so removed is ' " 'the musical cafe' " ' from the conceptual realm of the practical and even the amusing (a la berkeleyan brigade of the bourgeoisie). stalled by a little white lady named jean, whose pale eyelashes (the same translucent shade as her hair) reminded me of an aged poodle. we were unimpressed with each other, she offering me the same courtesy a lady would to her waiting girl-cum-protégé, and i smirking in petulant response. do not expect to get the job, though manager Noname seemed to like me. sisters in winged eyeliner, we are: feathered paint taunting brown skin. the painted ladies to jean's canid flatulence.

is Noname god? certainly she is paucity in the wake of paucity, but in an age of unsalvageable repentance can the prayers of few—expansive, timorous, and in octagonal rhyme though they may be—save hoi polloi? today the BART is filled with children in floral print and lace stockings (such as those of green gables, which i never grew). supple squeals sound the warning of complacency: to what do their fertilized worlds turn? which one of us can claim to be holy in these sea-green times? shit-filled time with nothing but stink and grubby pleasures. i wear a bralette the same shade of rose as her toothpick legs and my eyes, pregnant with crustacean corpses, pinch with droplets the taste of justice inarticulate. better this evacuation than kanye's futuristic "i": the illusion of subjective coherence, as if there were a time and a place for a Name. the truest lie, untempted by the parabolic nonsense of NOW. phallic jouissance NOW it NOW NOW NOW NOW NOW i make NOW up / down / around / (NOW) thing NOW NOW NOW [made (NOW)], k? you know?

delta kappa threnody (anthem of the police state)

have i ever told you about the time Y called the police on me? this is one of my most popular stories. by self-appointment: the shock value of the collision between sex, the public, and state discipline is arresting. literally, but not literarily; an illegible move by an otherwise legible girl, certainly not. we have no time to entertain the full anticipation of curiosity, so i start with a yield and the finish: have i ever told you about the time the police overheard me having sex? loud sex is gauche unwittingly inviting witnesses to a laborious performance of public passion is an exponent of the aforementioned gauche. knowing that the subject of the gaze is in fact not a subject at all but the impersonal gaze of the state-as-voyeur—the most abstracted incar(n/cer)ation of the polis—is not an exponent but a negative square root, or C-sharp minor, or a pentatonic dissension in opposition to the gauche. which is to say it is really like the graph of a natural logarithm, disoriented just enough to obscure the possibility of a felicitous coordinate, or a natural progression toward G major, or a diatonic resolution.

another time i start from the middle, when the highway gave way to liquid lanes and the inner city haze turned glassy like a roman noblewoman's morning toilet. frozen swirls and glossy stares all around, and oh he had a roman nose, did i mention that? but he was rolling where his nose was not, white powder that dusted freckles and already dulled bambi eyes. i inhale deeply and sneeze chalky excess across terrain more dim but less treacherous than midnight sahara, and somewhere across the world Y felt the shiver of a rattlesnake scale like teeth against glass, so he called the police. i tell you when i knew my secret had been so surreptitiously sliced open: door stilled by the pink barrel of man, who said my name too heavily, and from here the details get murky, something about smooth-talking suburban kids and the slippery privilege of light skin and shame and furtive phone calls. then, under the flickering light of frat row's finest—street lamps that never sleep—walking by water spilled through metal arms, above evaporating concrete that welcomes cohabitation. so that the precise functions of the hydrosphere, particularly where the evasive, ephemeral, and especially the vapid were concerned, are guarded by the rubber flotilla of the polis's finest, for whom the weight of sound had been amputated to afford the allure of an arched back. from duplicitous to serene: the police.

so basically, to wrap up the story, i lean with ease—too much ease?—into postcoital banter with the man of all men and i find that he's brought his friends and they'd been there for half an hour. polees. the implications are ripe for the picking but luckily i'm walking on air, or so i think, so the detonation of pulpy flesh and split skin doesn't even hit me, i just take a deeper breath of concrete vapor and we both deal with the repercussions of our actions, i to Y's dank smelling car and they to the quiet of exhaust. i wonder if my moans haunt the crisp dawn wind; otherwise, do they think of me at night when they collapse on our mother and surrender her to whispering plains? to each her own. when light again heats the porous grey, they hear a wailing from the shower, but, energized by the memory of eager groans, they convince themselves it is only an echo they concocted from monotony, tempered by steamy sweetness and the blink of wavering blue light.

(b)oink oink

do you remember that book *cybergirls* or whatever-the-fuck. for the unawares: a piece of teen fiction, peak popularity circa 2010—anno domini, in the time of eighth grade, when everything happened on aol. that is, the only way i can proffer my thoughts. this day stuck in low-res, low-function joke channel, without skin-tone-specific emojis and descriptors for all two hundred and fifty-six things i could be doing, without actually doing them. how do you know what i say is real?

taste of two-million-dollar reverie, or: piece of chocolate hugged by molars. last strip melting off crown, as if it were never there. so coolly does polish gleam yellow specter, as if darkness were not just awash, as if the only thing my tongue can remember is the taste of sweet water and arid hills. a gulp of two-million-dollar reverie, unkempt; none of the skyline.

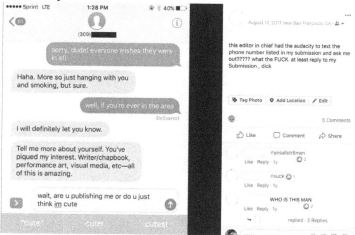

are white men with beards essentially creepy? it must not be: when he stares at me it is as if i am being swallowed by a cave and i can no longer embrace the wet darkness. where has the yonic gone, such that he decides not only my enjoyment but the very spectacle of my enjoyment, such that he owns my desire and the very act of desiring. two hundred thousand pixels and a rejection letter. white men with beards and a private instagram account. this is the way it goes, but, how did i know that to follow is not friendship, is not the fervor of editorial commitment. so yellow am i, off-white gleaming dully like salted flesh left to dry. oink oink.

bleeding fuchsia, i am sure he imagines. pussy like mango, not rose, but—rotten to the core, so he keeps his distance: only imagines through the computer screen, and when it gets to be too much two hundred thousand becomes two hundred until i am just a speck; a semicolon; a parenthesis. just a clue: a winky face. i say oink oink the pig deserves better. than to be your mascot. the irony: piggies to the pen, indeed, but no one called for the assault by the lasso, the butcher's knife. little piggies inside all of us deserve the sweet stink of shit, unless you are not a pig but: a white man with a beard.

mother pig births litter in the trough of my chest. nipples erect, flush with milk, but the man with the beard sees only the white specter of profit. discards shit for the still-soft wound of a mother's mouth. dark cave that opens at the suggestion of blade so that granite no longer looks like stone but gore, so grand the spectacle! what sex-filled stories to write.

fuck you, my friend tells me to say. *fuck you*, but i would have done that already if i wanted to. if you could only get a clue, or a needle. sew slice with the precision of a poem, but, shit-stained, granite grows infected until not even the smell of roasted flesh (chunks of pigs' blood the color of rich cacao, tossed lightly with olive oil) can proffer the blade to flicker at the wrist. little piggies inside all of us deserve to be butchered; broken molars, salt drying flesh.

lessons for burial

i decayed in the present tense. which is to say—what, actually? except the sigh of my sphincter, i am unoccupied with destiny. sure, we all die, but how does one tell the present with facts from the future? lest the future precedes the present, which it often does, and it is the past that we mistakenly look toward. as a position of inscrutability: a margin almost beside the point, literally and not literarily. there's no there-there. only a fading dawn.

today was the day i died. yesterday began with a ray and today continues with the mist. past tense tentative, i am not sure i am even an "i," or more accurately, if i am paralyzed in limbo until yesterday and tomorrow cohere. it is quickly becoming a day other than the one to which we turn, so i must have made known—past tense tentative—the event of my . . . well, what, exactly, i am unsure. there are no words which can be accurately contaminated by my situation: the microcosm of the diseased in a few letters? what is the name for a configuration of the Real in which form constitutes the whole and essence of content? in that sense there's no word for microcosm in the wake of my dawn's decay.

they say that death is sluggish, and i am here to confirm that the moment itself is anything, but, all moments afterward are exactly that. i am unsure why the people are so concerned with the method of my death; why it never crosses their mind to ask the mode of my decay, or everything that happens after. why they seem to think there is an "after." in the wake—well, there is no wakening for this. from this. sluggish is the right word to hold the jelly of my blood and the soft mucus of my flesh, as artefact. i am content to lie here while my insides pool out from beneath me, and i am content to observe the dissolution that makes me.

the most important moments of my life have been left in a miniature coffin you will find on the top right shelf of my desk. in it you will find the material equivalent of a corpse. i want you to take all of the objects—beware the sharp points of the pentagram—and burn it by the nearest body of water you can find. make sure nothing remains except ashes, and then take this paper to roll. inhale deeply to whisper me into rest.

taxonomy

4 once upon a time there was a girl named E. there was no one she loved in all the world better than her friend T. E and T believed that in each other's presence, only the marvelous could shine, rain or. T and E believed

7 —forget. she could, nonetheless.

3 the rain stopped, and she put herself to sleep. when the milk at the bottom of the glass turned translucent and became dewy drops glittering on the cusp, she knew that.

2 they lived love sweeter than adrenaline. a love built on unrelenting gaze and synchronized fear of failure, so T and E relished and resisted the other's touch.

6 a conflict in the body text, so she dissolved into floating alphabets punctuated by the occasional em-dash, but it was all she could do.

5 the particularity of their naiveté, the way in which they trusted so studiously, stupidly, in the absolution of their savior, or tempted the slippery hand of fate by believing that something, *something* good was destined to come.

1 the institution of death is the only one wherein unrelenting mediocrity may find a place.

8 but without absolution

notes from the plot

here lies the body text (née body/text, body-text). grammatical configuration between flesh and command, or thing and the thing that compelled it to action. today and all days from today there will be no truth in action because there will be no action, and there will be no more truths that carry prophecies. as verbs turn to adjectives to cloak cobwebs and the sweet stench of corpse, it is wondered if the dead can speak. only with a limp of accent and elided consonants. (it is me who is writing what i am writing. and i swear that this book is composed without words: like a mute photograph. this book is a silence: an interrogation.) soon we taste the resin of dirt in the crevice of sentences and crooked teeth, like stained english, or a language spent among sailors and mingled with the undertone of salt and sand. a language of kelpy excess, or the ocean is a giant grave, where body becomes feed, and text becomes vapor and the gravitational pull of the moon. (the word must not be adorned and become aesthetically worthless; it must be simply itself. with stiff, contaminated fingers, i must touch the invisible in its own squalor.) commas to the body text what fingers are to you and i, stretching vertically toward the sliver of dirt not yet contaminated by light. 'the hands are the first to go, until they become little more than nubs,' the body text a severed head, or an unruly ball of tumble seaweed. skid along wave tops until land on land like ending, or decapitation. "can the body text be freed from its sentence." not unless body/text a eulogy for the fish, or body/text the bodhisattva's robes. (i can no longer bear) the text, or the last thing left covering bones, (the routine of my existence, and) body, or mongrel, or text, or mongoloid floating, the sea is the color of urine (, were it not for the constant novelty of writing) (i should die) to be buried in quilt, knit by the letter c, autopsy conducted by the needle or curved scalpel, teeth harvested by scythe and then (symbolically) scattered into the scene. the seen.

part II: the sea after

a story in four reviews

for years, she had dreamt of him, so that when they finally met again, the quality of the experience was nothing short of surreal. it had happened without warning. one morning, she was taking her coffee, scrolling through her phone, when his face appeared: freshly cut, in her mind. she shook her head, tired, by now, of its million static frizzes. but she looked again, and there he was, out of her mind's eye and on the flickering screen. his name, in bold print, was enough to send a spasmodic wave of shivers down her spine. but before she could look away, she spotted that infelicitous article to which his name was attached. A REVIEW, it read, OF S'S DEBUT ESSAY COLLECTION. and her name—all its incongruous consonants and hyphenated surnames, appeared—so that even before she could think to escape, she became frozen. she sat still, eyes darting back and forth. first rage, then regret, filled her as she read his lilting words. the same hand as she remembered, full of lofty ideas and quizzical turns that could be taken for mocking comedy. so he had not liked it. but when they had last met, she had just begun work on the book. she had told him, over stuffed pimento, of her confusion, her hesitance, and above all, her doubt, that such metafictional reposes were worth such painstaking examination. he had had been friendly—warm, almost—and had offered her gentle smiles and probing questions, which, she had thought at the time, demonstrated interest and genuine curiosity. interest remained, perhaps, but curiosity, evidently not, as he derided her pages for their prosaic quality; the chaos of her imagination; the anger with which she infused her heady sentences—distressingly unreadable, he had written. or, not worth being understood.

this last part hurt her the most, for, in her dreams, he still appeared to her as the exuberant nineteen-year-old he had been. how, with his slender fingers, he could animate an idea! and the slight pucker of his lips, as he articulated (with what precision!) an idea—of physics, roman philosophy, the neapolitan war—that she could not yet understand. he had illuminated the path of the not-yet-comprehensible; she, in turn, had failed to do the same.

days later, she received a cordial email from him. *how are you?* he had written, after all this time. and, in a somewhat remorseful tone, he congratulated her on the publication of her book. *how difficult it is to get published in this economy*, he mused. *for that, you should be very proud.* she shook her head sadly. at the closing, he dared to ask, with not a mite of trepidation, if she was in new york; that he had read she was, and if so, would she like to get a coffee sometime? what for, she thought bitterly, so that the critic and his object of criticism could be reunited in that subject/object relationship they had simulated all those years ago?

once, in the midst of their affair, he had invited her to his parents' ranch in santa barbara. his mother, a gifted equestrienne, had a stable of purebreds with whom he had never felt a connection. so he had explained; *but you like to ride, yes?* he asked. she had gone, more out of obligation to the insinuation of a sexual escapade than desire to relish the extravagance of his sizeable inheritance. they were not together, then; they had never truly been together. on the morning of her departure, the stable hand caught them kissing at the breakfast table. she remembered the way he had startled, then drew back. *this is my friend*, he had muttered to the man, not looking at her. hired help, meet hired help, she had written angrily in a fictionalized account of the incident. but it was perhaps unfair, for wasn't it true that he had repeated often, through the course of their relationship, that there was to be no promises, no expectations? until she, too, became afraid of commitment and learned to enjoy him in the fullness of his ephemerality, finally trapping him within the chaos of her memory, where he remained forever in sight, just out of touch.

she deleted the email, changed her mind, then took a screenshot of the text to be woven into a visual piece on which she was at work. burial, meet body, she would title the project, to little acclaim. then, with the same vigor with which she had held onto that last scrap of him, she forgot him. to my knowledge, they never met again.

REVIEW ONE (editor's note: *felt pen and paper collage*)

REVIEW TWO (editor's note: *excerpt of an unpublished essay by S titled "beyond the autobiographical"*)

there are certain kinds of sorrow which lose their humanity once exposed. for this reason, a story is a weapon insofar as it promises to uncover, transcend, manifest. these days, she was in pursuit of an untranslatable grief. perhaps it's a subaltern's grief, a subterranean wavelength whose echoes can neither be heard nor understood; a grief, which, in turn, condemns the griever to the stations of irrationality; hysteria; weakness. in short, she is consumed by a feminine grief—a sorrow turned sour by its attachment, a melancholy queerly befitting the crimes of womanhood. if, at the heart of every failure and its concomitant sorrow lies a perpetrator and a cause, the circuits of gendered grief possess no single villain nor transcript of injury. there's no event, but an archive of grief, whose unspeakable language obscures the circuit of impact until there are only shadows in its wake. the language of shadows is the tongue of elena ferrante.

tracing the lives of two italian girls through the dawn of girlhood to the dusk of solitude, ferrante's neapolitan series is a confessional tome whose excesses spill past boundaries of speaker and spoken. at times unapologetically sentimental, and others cruelly objective, the text is the only body who materializes, in and through a chain of proxies at the end of which sits the author herself, illegible beneath the cloak of her pseudonym. those who have grieved know: where the intensity of grief propels a desire to reenact the veracity of pain, the moment of utterance is loaded with impossibilities. all fictions are in truth, lies, and all writers, liars. just as the author births narrative, her words, in turn, trap her, forcing her to make public what is essentially private; universal, what is irreducibly personal. the politics of seeing is a politics of distance, is a politics of truth—is it possible, ferrante challenges us to ask, to lay the trap of words, and slip out from underneath it all?

the neapolitan series is an illusion, and the truest confessional yet. the tangled web of touches is a body without organs, or, a body with too many organs, whose slime writes, manifests, then usurps the flesh. no more is the burden of autobiography; the translucent woman's soul. as if the language were a mask, ferrante leads the reader back to herself, so that she (and wherever she may be right now—behind the screen, tucked in the palimpsest of nostalgia, wound by the strand of the comma) were the one who penned the text, her body given bare to the creational tip of the textual scalpel. two thousand pages make a house of mirrors, so that whatever truth may be caught only glimmers in the scopophilic corridor of the seeing and the seen.

ferrante writes with a fearlessness that borders on the soft, as if she understands the unspoken terms of the scriptocentric agreement, but refuses to fall prey to the decrees of the sentence. it's not her flesh, or even the flesh of her characters which she bares to the hardness of the serif dagger. instead, the words themselves which comprise a knifefight: shielded by the cacophony of the metal wound, the wail of the unspeakable bares her ghostly ontology. perhaps it was joan didion who said, "we tell ourselves stories in order to live." she is no longer sure, for, despite quivering language, the fictions we tell ourselves fail. only, in the case of elena ferrante, failure is resignified as consummation, an ephemeral articulation toward which the subaltern takes us, comma by wretched comma until we are nothing but shadows, spilling out of the archive, tearing it asunder.

REVIEW THREE (editor's note: *felt pen and paper collage*)

REVIEW FOUR (editor's note: *excerpt from a scrapbook entry, captioned "it all comes back to what you know"*)

If words could speak, what secrets would they reveal? This is the central question underlining S's debut collection, *american symphony: other white lies*. Taking the form of a temporally distorted palimpsest, the essays, metafictional at one turn, observational at another, weave an archive of solipsistic madness. Lest it be rude to dismiss the inner workings of a mind as madness, S seems to want us to do just that. Her words flow erratically from one page to another, tearing the stitches of genre until creative nonfiction becomes . . . flash fiction, or memoir, or some variation of crea/fic/tive/non/tion. But the creative is nowhere to be found, having left only disorder in its wake.

Citing the cannon of women confessional writers from Sylvia Plath to Elena Ferrante, of whom she claims to be an ardent fan, S puts her own spin on the racialized truth-telling that she calls her life's project. "storied daughters and woven breasts, i make nothing up," she writes, "only pull loose clench of yarn by way of caressing you." But if it is the illusory touch that is her objective, S has failed. Her writing, at times, veers into the sharply pedantic, or she becomes too invested in her own narrative, spinning sentences in lieu of substance, leaving the reader (and, one may fear, herself) spinning in the chaos of uncertain ideas.

Just as ideas are not created equally, neither are feelings. But feelings—the grief of betrayal, the desire of return, the ennui of misdirection—are what drive the central movement of S's work. Where Elena Ferrante manages to draw the reader into a richly woven web of lies (demonstrating, once more, the veracity of her characters' emotional interiority), S leaves us behind, grasping at traces of intertextual continuity that feel more like fog than rain. elsewhere, she writes,

> touching cheek and yanking your nose, fingers slipping hair matchstick rustle. dissolving you or—devouring you by sight. to pull you closer, like she fists loose-leaf: nothing made, up another paper crown ashy lips colored in one sepia-toned breath. everything so dark, so pitch black but . . . so hard. porcelain without life, like this, exorcism a la luxury of self-invention, and, i don't make anything up, except the story of my life, so bright it touched your life.

But who is porcelain? Who is ashy? And what, exactly, of her life has S revealed, to the worthiness of touching? The detached jumble of signifiers makes certain that S will never be understood, and that, it is possible, she herself doesn't even understand. There are great writers, and there are good writers. Then, there are writers who write for the sake of writing, without feeling for the nerve endings of words, the gentle breath of the comma. S belongs in the latter category, with her unending sentences and explosive feelings. One gets the sense that she has too much to tell you; that she is convinced you will never understand; and that, principally, she is frustrated, though with whom it is unclear. To that, the literary world says: enough! If a writer is unconvinced of the meaning she conveys, then she has no business writing. Perhaps equally important, there are some feelings not worth discussing. What was it that Socrates said, by way of Thumper? If you can't say something nice, don't say nothin' at all. It is a lesson from which we would all benefit, S most of all.

procedures a/b

she felt as if she were walking on air. the train had arrived on schedule in rome that afternoon. not a single ray of light shone through the damp sky, to which she shouted, grey! grey! grey! but she was not grey, only a monochrome yellow, the absence of a sun which she had sucked into her sternum. "don't come back," he had told her. but integrity was the essential element which she lacked. "don't come back," she thought to herself, but there was already no way of returning. how do you recover that which is irrevocably lost? "what if," she had told him earlier that day, "we are not the right one for each other?" you need me more than i need you, was what she wanted to say. you want me in ways of which i can't possibly conceive, and i will never want you the same way. but even as she typed those words, feeling with clarity that she was making a mistake for which she would suffer dearly, she could not help but soar, instead of sink. she arrived at the station in a state of exuberant ennui. no, she did not need him, she told herself. his words echoed in her mind. "come back to me today," he had said. "why are you going to venice? why, when there is someone here who wants you, so much." this had scared her; she was in danger of falling into his orbit. she could feel her gears shifting backward, her heart becoming smaller as she swallowed the blood which spurt forth. she did not know what she wanted, and, in the absence of stars, there were none to guide her out of the twinkling void into which she had succumbed.

she remembered that milan felt like spring. everywhere, the clatter of goodbyes. if you stay in any place long enough, everything becomes a story, she quoted to herself. the only goodbyes were in jest, but her story had no jest, only a cloying melancholia which propelled her ever forward into the wet canvas of her heart. pure black, with a slash haphazardly dividing it in two—this was the canvass of her heart. only, unlike the violent trough which divided llucio fontana's feminine corpses, her gash was not the imagined yearning of a penetrative thrust, but an invisible clitoral vibration always already disappearing, reemerging. her pussy was made of iron, but they always wanted to fuck with a knife.

as if her body had a mind of its own (*how funny to be a spectator of your own life*, she thought), she made her way to the metro, then turned and walked back to the ticket office. *could i buy a ticket to milan, please,* she said. in the crowd of deportees, the timeline of her life was spliced in two, as if for the first time, she possessed a semblance of a will.

a mistake—this is what you are making, she told herself, but she was so far away that the only sound her body could hear was an echo of an echo. "m ta ke," a whisper. she was forever declaring her true self, so that every self she had shown could be yanked beneath their feet. this was her way of staying afloat, which is to say, it was necessary for her to evacuate herself, continuously, vigorously, until there was nothing left, and she ceased to be anywhere else but there. on the horizon of comprehension—where the most exciting excavation could be made, for she was an artifact begging to be known. desperate, she knew, for the right scalpel to cut through the dust of her flesh, straight into empty sternum, crumbling, crumbling.

PROCEDURE B

she heard the patter of feet, and then he emerged. seeing him never failed to shock her: a contrast of curves and angles humanized the mechanical fluidity with which he moved. almost as if he were not quite there, so close did he shrink to the ground, peering out at her from the expanse of his smooth pate. they greeted each other with a gentle kiss. outside, it snowed lightly, and she, dotted with pinpricks from the cold, shuddered into the embrace. was he upset at her? she never knew. in the midst of lovemaking he would sometimes stare into her eyes, as if seeing her for the first time, and sigh. *bellissima*, he would whisper. or, *molto bene*, and she would sink deeper into him, until all she could see were the coal black of his eyes, quivering beneath feathery lashes.

"i like you better when you are soft," he told her as he made her coffee. *how trite,* she thought. she made no sound. "like this morning, for example," he continued, "you were so sweet. i could imagine spending my life with you." *half asleep, you mean,* she thought. *half a human, with my consciousness dimmed.* but of course, he did not mean it that way, ! reproached herself. her mother had often suggested, in her gentle way, that emotional compromise was necessary to a functional love. by which, ! knew, she meant that it took many lies for a marriage to work. performance and selective memory: she was adept at both, and the sentence of the love story required that she always be on her feet. but she had given up theater long ago, convinced that the stage was better set on the street, that it was less the craft of insertion which she valued than a permanent readiness for the Marvelous. she wondered how the Césaires micro-managed their partnership (was it a romance?). for example, did they copulate often in the late years of their marriage?

on a different occasion, he had said, too, that he hated all forms of pretense. "don't say bullshit," he would reprimand when he felt that she (or was it some trace of her—eyes, mouth, the cartilage of her elbow mid-gesture) was being insincere. by now she knew the circuitry of his anxiety like the etchings on her palm. in the peak moments of his distress, he needed all of her—or, he needed her ready in action, open like a petal for lucid access. she would oil her gears with chapped hands and open for him in the way that she could, mistaking orifice for the mute canvas of a soul. but what he wanted was for her to slice herself apart for him: he was no killer, only, tormented by the desires of one, he pleaded with her to perform the actions he could not bring himself to do. so that he could lick the wounds she had manifested for him, this was the best they could manage: fist straining against bruised metal. she had hidden all the knives.

they barely had sex now, so tired did she feel from his constant berating, and he, hurt by her sudden explosions. "you revolutionary," he used to whisper to her in the aftermath of their tousling. "cosi buona, mia bella." in the heat of their crises, he would murmur (eyes lingering), *you have a man inside of you.* faced with her emotive excess, he attempted the facade of rationality; a gauze, he thought, for oozing pus. but if misinformation were a wound, hers would be a rash, cutting fire across the expanse of her mouth. she did not bleed—her fire came from a well deeper than the cheap hemoglobin she served to him as soup. he wanted a piece of her flesh, but how could she explain to him that none, not even she, could dissolve the coppery plastic of her veins? her mechanical resistance did the unexpected: one moment, they electrified him from the misdirection of his wallowing; otherwise, they barricaded him with a strength against which he could not compete.

one day, he woke to a pile of gears at the foot of his bed. *!?*, he reached for her, but in the space where she had been, he found only the smooth expanse of the blanket, damp with the trace of something wet. he lifted the cover to kick warm air for reassurance of flesh. he found, instead, a gaping slash where a face had been. the stale smell of lavender oozed from the depth of the slim cavern. cautiously, with his eyes closed, he felt the ribbed gooseflesh of its edges. a moan sounded (from his chest, he wondered), and lingered until all that he could hear was the slosh of thumping sinking deeper, deeper into the cotton expanse through which she had disappeared.

12 million dollars, free childcare, and a diaper to boot, after carmen machado (editor's note: unpublished essay, after *The Return of Superman*, ep. 181)

episode X – the twins are addicted to the smart phones [cameras rolling]

the twins are curled up on the couch, quieter than ever. in their hands, they clutch the silver platelet—their object of attention. father hwi-jae walks in: "you guys have been watching videos for too long . . . it will ruin your eyesight." he tells them that they must find something else with which to entertain themselves. they nod, hands still wrapped around the phone. later, youngest seo-jun sneaks onto hwi-jae's phone while no one's around, but finds that the phone is locked. he accidentally takes a photo of himself: the culprit, found. undeterred, hwi-jae sets an hourglass timer. "you can play for ten minutes," he tells his sons. "trust us," they reply. they keep their promise, and as a reward, hwi-jae sends them to the supermarket to buy some snacks. but on the way back, the desire strikes again. they stop at a cafe, and borrow the shopkeeper's phone. "what took you so long?" hwi-jae asks. "we accidentally used a smartphone," seo-eon replies, forlorn. "sorry, dad." as a final measure, hwi-jae calls up a policeman buddy. "yes, hello," he says, "i'm the father of seo-eon and seo-jun." "ah, yes," the friend replies. "we've just received a special report, of a pair of five-year-old twins who keep asking for a smartphone with which to watch videos. it's a serious problem for their eyesight." "what should i do?" hwi-jae asks. "first, give up your smartphone, so they can break the habit," the order arrives. hwi-jae does as he's told. the twins break into tears simultaneously. the phone is deactivated. lesson learned.

episode X – the twins find money. will they return it?
[cameras rolling]
the twins are sent to play in the neighborhood playground while hwi-jae runs an errand. they meet a ginger cat, tumble down the slide, and hop through a caterpillar balancing course. just as he is about to finish, seo-eon discovers a thousand won bill fluttering beneath the caterpillar's metal stomach. "what should we do?" he asks seo-jun. "can i just keep it? we can buy chocolate bread with it." "it's not ours," seo-jun replies. "that's a no-no." after discussion, the twins decide to return the bill to the bank, where, they note, is where people bring money. "you can take this to the police station," the bank teller tells them. "they will find the owner of the money." just then, hwi-jae returns from the errand. "you've done well," he tells his boys. "if you ever find money, you can return it to the police station." as a reward for their honesty, the boys receive plastic whistles from the police officer. they blow hard, before hwi-jae leads them in a salute.

episode X – the twins dropped something during an errand
[cameras rolling]
the twins have been sent to recycle thirty-five empty milk containers at the community center in exchange for a roll of toilet paper. cameras start flashing as soon as they arrive, but everyone is kind and attentive to them. seo-eon takes the toilet paper proudly, and the twins head into the children's library next door, trailed by a team of cameras. "should we have a competition to see who can find the most dinosaur books?" seo-eon asks seo-jun, who nods. after each twin has found six dinosaur books, they clean up and leave the library. "let's go eat bread," seo-jun says. the brothers hold hands as they scramble up the stairs to the neighborhood bakery, where they

share red bean bread and a tray of chocolate muffins. "should we play a quiz game?" seo-jun asks seo-eon. "i'll ask the first question." they play three rounds, and then head to the playground. just then, sco-jun grows solemn. "where did the toilet paper go?" he asks seo-eon. "oh no, we left it behind," seo-eon replies. "i should have taken care of it." after debate, they decide it's impossible to find the toilet paper, so they head to the convenience store to buy another roll. "dad, we lost the toilet paper," they tell hwi-jae after returning home. "we thought you'd get mad, so we bought some more." hwi-jae looks stern for a second. "it's okay, but don't lose important things," he tells them. "you've done well, boys."

episode X – the twins have to live apart
[cameras rolling]
the twins are fighting again. in desperation, hwi-jae hatches a plan: he calls his wife and makes the preparations. while he plays spin the tops with seo-eon, his wife quietly slips away with seo-jun to a local café. after a while, seo-eon grows restless. "where's seo-jun?" he asks. "who's sco-jun?" hwi-jae asks. "we were born together," seo-eon answers, his voice cracking. "we came from mom's stomach together." finally, hwi-jae reveals the truth. "because the two of you fight so much, only one of you will live with mom and i. we've sent seo-jun to live with your aunt in vietnam." seo-eon immediately breaks into tears. at the café, mom buys seo-jun a slice of chocolate cake. "where's seo-eon?" seo-jun asks. mom reveals that seo-eon has been sent to the united states, as a remedy for the twin's constant fighting. when his pleas to bring seo-eon back don't work, seo-jun's pout turns into tears. "i want to live with him," he cries. "twins should be together." even the chocolate cake can't console him. "can seo-eon eat this in the united states?" he asks. when the twins are reunited at a park, they run toward each other with the fervor of friends. seo-eon offers seo-jun ice cream, and they embrace. a touching scene of brotherly love.

episode X – the twins find a smartphone
[cameras rolling]
hwi-jae takes the boys to a blood center, where he will be
donating blood. the boys are worried, but hwi-jae assures them
that everything will be okay, and sends them to buy bread
while he prepares to get blood drawn. "let's go play at the claw
machine," seo-jun says. they race to the machine, and, after
three tries and a prayer, fail to grab a pokémon doll. resigned,
they decide to buy a snack instead. as they drink mango juice
on a sofa of the mall, they hear a strange chirping. near them,
an abandoned cell phone vibrates. "look at this," seo-jun says.
"whose is that?" seo-eon asks. they contemplate leaving the
phone behind, but realize that someone else might take it. just
then, the phone rings again. "hello?" seo-eon answers. "is this
your mobile phone? why did you leave it here?" "yes, this is
my phone," a flustered man on the other end answers. "are
you a student?" "what's that?" seo-eon asks. "we are two five-
year-olds." after some confused banter, they agree to meet at
the claw machine on the fourth floor of the mall. a relieved
man in a suit greets them. he pats them on the head, and asks
the producers if he will be on tape. he offers to buy the twins
an ice cream, but seo-eon requests a toy. when hwi-jae finds
them again, the boys are clutching pikachu dolls and bursting
to tell him the story. "oh, so he bought you the toy as a token
of thanks? you've done well, my boys," hwi-jae says.

episode X – the twins sing at Gayo Stage
[cameras rolling]
hwi-jae's father is sick with alzheimer's disease. as a surprise,
hwi-jae and the twins prepare to sing a song dedicated to him
at Gayo Stage, a popular senior show on MBC. they meet the
host of the show, who asks them to sign a play contract, and
hands them fifty thousand won each as payment. their first
paid gig, if we discount the $4.25 million they are worth in
endorsements alone. the performance, a rendition of "cha cha

cha together," is completed without a glitch. in their matching backpacks, the twins are miniatures of hwi-jae, who hops around with the vigor of a show host in his plaid suit. later, at their grandfather's house, hwi-jae proudly plays the segment. "do you know who that is?" he asks. "no," elder lee replies. "are you sure?" hwi-jae asks again. "you're not playing around with me, right?" when it's clear that his father's alzheimer's has progressed so far that he truly can't recognize his son and grandsons on television, hwi-jae cups his head in his hands. he puts his father to bed, and leans against the window, crying. "what are you doing, dad?" seo-eon asks. "nothing, i'm fine," comes the reply. nonetheless, seo-eon runs up to hwi-jae and to look out the window next to his father, silent.

and then where did she go?

when she first found out about the baby, S almost fainted. she had first felt a tingle in her lower abdomen, a sign which she took to mean that the flower was blooming, or her period was coming. the next day, during her run, a tiny voice had sounded, almost imperceptibly, in her ear. *mama*, it crooned. she startled, and almost ran off the trail. "who is this," she hissed. "who gave you permission to claim me as your mama." but the voice remained tactfully mum, and she dismissed the incident warily. that evening, she confronted her girlfriend with an unusual sincerity that caused the other to wonder if indeed S had finally suffered a nervous breakdown. "P," S had murmured, "what would you do if i became pregnant?" what, how, with whom, the reply had come. though the hard facts of biology had shifted to make way for possibility, they had been ambivalent with contraceptive use, convinced that in the absence of desire, nothing could foment. on the contrary, theirs was a relationship founded on the anti-reproductive genealogy of gay and lesbian activism of the late twentieth century, a phenomenon which long preceded them, but to which both clung with an unquestioning nostalgia. "i don't know," S had finally answered. "just, what if?" don't be silly, P said. *yes, be silly*, the small voice in her ear countered.

when S began throwing up daily after breakfast, P grew worried that something had indeed happened. if not a psychological crisis, then perhaps an incident of infidelity, or an act of sabotage by S herself. she had read somewhere that phantom pregnancies, a folklore of the twentieth century, were still possible, causing desiring mothers to experience all the false promises of parturiency with none of the fruits. perhaps that was what S suffered from, though P wondered to herself when the idea of child had struck her partner, and how she had been ignorant of its entrance into their lives. made anxious by uncertainty, P accompanied S to the gynecologist, who declared her healthy, save a slight yeast infection for which she prescribed an antibiotic. "any unusual stress in your life?" she asked S, who shook her head. "it's not uncommon for women your age to experience bouts of nausea accompanied by symptoms of pregnancy. it's the body's way of asserting its natural cycle, though in this day and age, such notions as 'natural' are all but disappearing!" P rolled her eyes. that night, she lay her head on S's stomach, and rubbed it with the tenderness of a ripe peach. "maybe a baby wouldn't be so bad," she whispered. S said nothing, only stroked P's thin locks with a contemplativeness she had not felt since she was a young girl.

S took on the habit of sleeping with ear plugs. nightly, the little voice returned to her in wails. *hello, i'm hungry,* it cried one night, and on another, *hello, why don't you want me?* S tried to shut out the voice with eyes clenched, but no matter how she tried, the temptation of communication with this foreign body, inundated with raw need, clutched a corner of her heart. "who are you," she whispered once. "who gave you permission to make home in my body." how could she explain that the only life she could offer was of torn flesh and unblinking precarity. a child deserved someone dependable, not one who could barely retain the boundaries of her body. perhaps it was in reaction to this anxiety about porous boundaries and eliding distinctions that S began to fear and hate her baby.

whenever she spoke back to the spark, she was met with an eerie silence. as if, in the absence of a response, the voice was waging its own campaign of resistance. "we didn't choose each other," S told it, "so please leave." but leave it did not, until one day, several months after the initial whisper, the voice returned with a serious proclamation. *hello---*, it said, and this time S was startled into inaction by the lucidity of its voice, the audacious act of naming. *what is life in the absence of living?* S rushed to the bathroom, where she released the contents of that day's lunch. i really must be going crazy, she thought to herself. that evening, as she and P prepared for bed, a pang sounded in her abdomen. she gave a cry and P looked up, concerned. S bent over, clutching at the soft tissue that joined rib to hip. "darling, you're bleeding," P cried. on the seat of S's trousers, a crimson blot slowly unfurled. S did not reply. agony blinded her periphery, until all she could see were the edges of P's feet, crouched next to her as arms held her falling body against the bed. P's shouts became a murmur, and as the pain overtook her, S closed her eyes. "where are you?" she thought. *we never chose each other,* the voice replied.

when S came to, she felt as if the hospital's fluorescent lights had bored a hole through her cranium. P sat next to her, a look of distress clouding her roguish features. "where are we," S murmured, closing her eyes again. "the hospital, baby, "P whispered. "you had a ruptured fallopian tube." S sighed. then, eyes fluttering open, "what's in a life lost?" "what life, darling," P asked. S noted that with her eyebrows scrunched, P resembled a version of her younger brother. she smiled and offered a hand to P's cheek. "she released me, i heard her voice." P returned the smile with uncertainty. "how are you feeling now?" S shook her head. "she was here, she closed her eyes, and she was beautiful as she passed through me."

later, a worried P consulted the doctor. "sometimes," the gynecologist explained, "it's natural for one member of a female homosexual couple to feel intense desire for reproduction. that, combined with your partner's preexisting condition, can cause undue stress on the reproductive system. some rest will be good for her. and you may want to consider child-rearing—it may be the best thing for her, next to full-fledged, natural motherhood." the woman's grey hair was parted in the middle, spilling onto a crocheted sweater. the sweater bore a distinct mahogany color, and was dotted at random intervals with clumps of fabric that bore the color of a runny line of snot. together, the colors produced a heightening effect on the grey woman's already incongruous figure, which was now coated as if a chillingly steep mountain, through whose earth spurted eruptions of pus.

P clenched her teeth and said nothing. the next morning, she returned to S's room with a bouquet of orange daffodils.

★★★

somewhere in the ether, the spirit of S's love child rose to form. *some people are not fit to be mothers,* it whispered. a crowd leaned in around it, translucent forms shimmering in the light. *and some,* the ghost child continued, *are bodies unfit for colonization. they may confuse the pull of dependence for love, or the threat of dissolution for stability. such was the woman i have just left.* the hollow listeners shivered with antagonism. some departed at the sound of the speaker's cynicism. others drew in closer. *motherhood is an outdated principle,* the spirit proceeded. its subterranean voice wavered with the weight of its truth. *when you reside in a body of flesh, you ask her to become one with you. sometimes, the truth-value of synthesis is too great for us to bear. there is too much to be absorbed, or too little to be abolished. ironically, it is always the best would-be mothers who ask us to withhold our consumptive presence. they can't afford to vivisect their souls just yet—there is too much that will spill into the child, and we are the ones who must wager with the burden of excess. a life that becomes trodden by the impossible puzzle of what it meant to live. such was the case of the woman i have just left.*

in the corner of the crowd, a glistening shadow sent a pang of sympathy, then raised its voice in question. *but some actively look to bear the fruit of the womb. they believe in the beauty of our synthesis, and seek it for purposes both narcissistic and selfless.* the crowd shimmered in agreement. spirit paused for a long moment. *it is true, there are those who welcome the joy of conception. perhaps with them, there is the possibility of a loving pregnancy—a willful absolution of self and a consensual union between body and souls. it can be a beautiful thing. even so, their fetishistic exaltation is no promise of a life. of those joyful pregnancies, how many are preceded by long stretches of internal ambivalence? how many are truly a decision made by will, untouched by the demanding arc of the invisible hand, in the name of Nature? how many,* the spirit intoned, *still threaten to overburden us with the excess of their repression? in an age of cyborgs and digital memory, which one of us is natural,* the spirit mused. *the domain of "motherhood" itself is a slippery signifier for which there is no translation.*

it was on a roll, now, and the edges of its consciousness glistened in the fervor of its proclamation. *the body we are sent to colonize is only a body, but the selective narrative of Nature has tasked it with being feminine; the Mother is asked to be both guardian and arbiter, a shell in which we might be protected, and an impossibly gendered flesh from which we take our meals. how are we to eat from a body who cannot feed itself? they have invented figures for an abstract explanation of excess: the Holy Body of Man, the sacrificial lamb, the Mother who gives her son to be killed in the name of payment. but who is the real recipient, and from whom does the sacrifice take its body? the attribution of sacrifice—itself an antidote to meaningless giving—is, somehow, a feminine principle, as is the rounded excess through whose delivery a "mother" is expected to transform herself. but what does it mean to "mother"?*

the spirit paused and looked out at the sea of opaque membranes, many of whom now shivered in syncopation—as if feeling the artificial coldness of their orphanage, the spirit thought. *is the approximation of touch not enough? must we become one, and in the process, consume the corpse of the host?* to that, none had an answer. soon after, the spirit descended again, this time to the womb of a wild boar, where it gestated in peace and, after it was born, escaped to the periphery of Life, where such theoretical questions bothered it no longer.

l'intercession

many years later, as the girl siphoned her inheritance to pose as a bohemian artist in the capital of europe, they met again. the sun was the color of rust in a coffee cup, and throngs of passersby obscured their view of each other at first. but when the crowd cleared, wobbling like a flock of pigeons, serena saw her, sitting across the plaza with half a cigarette dangling from her lips. she leaned toward the man next to her, made to whisper, and threw her head back in a laugh. it was a full laugh, with head tilted back and throat so full that serena thought she could catch a glimpse of the larynx's ridges. she looked the same as she did at eighteen, hair waving in the wind and her nose, crunched in the charming expression of the amused. serena took a sharp breath, slid on her sunglasses, and looked away. in the periphery of her lowered gaze, she could see the edge of a white tablecloth, above which lay a stack of thin pamphlets. the man was speaking now, and, as the girl glanced at him askance, he snuck a kiss on her neck. serena stood up. she dusted her chinos and smoothed her straw hat. on her feet, she towered over the cobblestones, but the girl made no notice of her. the man now stroked her knee, and she glanced back at him with a lingering gaze. a young woman approached the table, motioned to the pamphlets. serena observed the conversation, silent from afar, and noted the exchange of money, the unreserved joy with which the girl's face opened to her customer. serena's breath caught in her chest. she coughed. it had been long since she had felt this dull ache, but it seemed that where the mind forgot, the body could not. she tugged at her hat and strode over to the stand.

a torn hand-painted sign hung over the edge of the table,

whose cloth now fluttered in the dusk breeze. "aM can mpho Y," she made out. "7€ Ne, 10€ t O."

bonjour, the girl said. serena startled. she cleared her throat.

hello, welcome! the girl said, again. *would you like to take a look?* serena nodded.

a thick sheath of paper tucked between canvas covers, overlain with the title—the book she had talked about writing ("written about talking," she had said). that this book had weathered the years struck serena as incredible. where the eye deceives, text bears the changing past with an unforgiving gaze. serena wondered if the ink blot on her page was still there. some fleeting lines of prose came to her; she remembered the clean smell of daffodils, the wind, her hair clutched between wiry fingers. no, it was best not to look.

ah. she stiffened her back, and smiled politely. *merci beaucoup.* the girl looked at her, then shook her head ruefully.

pas de problème. take a card, she tilted her head. *bye now.*

Dear White Girl, Please Go Back Whence You Came (editor's note: unpublished short story)

during her college orientation, she had the unexpected pleasure of staying at a commune in the remote forest of western massachusetts. she had not expected it—one moment, she was asleep on the bus, the next moment, the loud voice of the program director awoke her to a gnome garden painted with psychedelic reds. we're here, he had shouted, with enough enthusiasm to stir the bleary-eyed teenagers to a semblance of curiosity. when she found, to her surprise, a haphazard village of sloping huts and a carefully overgrown orchard, she had felt as if a pixie during the summer of love. only, it was cold, and there was little love to be found save a crazed serenity, evident in the mushroom-cloud roofs and an aptly named acid house. the settlement, as it was now known, had been active since the beginning. the beginning, she learned, was what the white folk called their resistance—summer, and the subsequently short-lived fall, winter, and springs of protest. to what precise cause the act of this seclusion tended, she was unsure: some words coagulated together, like eco-sustainability, alternative socialities, undermining the authority of the state machine. it seemed that for the residents (travelers, they preferred to call themselves), everything was, or could be construed as, an act of defiance: rebellion in copulation; in celibacy; in marriage; in not-marriage; in children; in isolation; in urbanity; in every conceivable variation of the normative until even the normative, hazy through the multifocal lens of the silvery tab, seemed vaguely subversive.

they called the commune zomia, but it was less a constellation than a scramble. supposedly, there was an entire school of eastern teachings which not only justified, but extended, the term of this defiance; a school to which the residents of zomia had contributed significantly, and, they would add, would the young people like to buy a book. she was sure there was a guru somewhere, and though no one could find him, it occurred to her that perhaps they had lost him amongst the deer, or maybe he was, in fact, one of the gnomes in the garden, leading them through titillating green to the other side, wherever that may be. still, the image of the isolated village stood in her mind she referred back to it sporadically, and with great pleasure: perhaps one day, she, too, would be capable of throwing it all away and going to live a nomadic life, searching for spirituality in the wild, wild woods.

what "it" was, she never knew, nor did she ever possess enough to indulge in the satisfaction of disposal. nevertheless, the idea of such privileged seclusion clouded her mind, and she allowed herself the luxury of abstract imaginaries—in them, her body was never present, only a vague trace that she was experiencing communal living; she was in zomia's chilly forest; she might go back someday, form be damned. when one day, she awoke to find herself lying not in the three-hundred count sheets she had bought on sale, but a lumpy mattress that smelled of rain, she panicked. the room around her glowered in the yellow light of dawn; she felt a breeze enter through the window. but what window? she twisted her neck and heard it pop. pop, like the windowsill, which shuddered from the touch of the wind. she found in herself a curious sense of familiarity, and for a moment, felt a calming sense of stability. that ended, however, when she stood up and found herself facing, in the mirror by the end of the bed, a stranger whose features disgusted her. she let out a cry of surprise. the girl in front of her had straw hair, a sharp nose, and taut, pale skin which stretched tightly over her narrow face and invisible lips. she was, indisputably and distressingly, a ghost. she became convinced that she had died, and in the afterlife, was punished to reemerge through the frigid form of . . . she struggled to find the words. a white girl.

a knock sounded at the door, and a mousy woman peeked at her from behind the door frame. "good morning, margaret," she called out. "are you ready to help with breakfast?" she got up, numb, and put on a sweater. she had known this woman, years ago. it was the guru's most promising student, a zomia resident named barbara.

the rest of the day passed in such a fashion. she was greeted sporadically, and mostly left to her own devices. she found the old orchard, now untended and filled with dying buds. she stayed there for hours, in shock, staring up at the clear sky. in the evening, after the compulsory meditation exercise (during which she opened her eyes, and stared at the disheveled people around her—all equally pale, with a near absence of color), she discovered margaret's diary, tucked in a creaking floorboard next to the bed. she read slowly, growing increasingly alarmed. here was a girl whose thoughts almost paralleled hers, but who, after graduating with a degree in environmental studies, had chosen to live in seclusion at the commune, finishing a book of short stories imagining an eco-dystopian collapse coordinated by the virgin mary. two days ago, she had killed herself.

or so the diary had read. but that couldn't have been, for wasn't she margaret, now, in margaret's very body, which could not be dead if it were currently occupied by her? when she finally fell asleep, by the faint light of the morning, it was of her body that she dreamt, limbs contorted, as it was thrown into a shallow grave and buried.

she woke with a start. the sun shone brightly on her face, and through her squint she could see that the door had been left ajar. no doubt barbara had tried to call on her again this morning, but (thankfully) had left her to sleep. she made to dress, avoiding the mirror, but when she lifted her shirt, she discovered no longer the sickening pallor which had so frightened her, but the olive tan of her skin. her skin— and, she soon discovered, her hair, her eyes. she marveled at the limber ease with which she moved, once again, in her own body. it was then that she heard a commotion in the commons, and rushed out of the room, shirt still half undone.

a tightly knit circle had gathered on one end of the hall. she spotted barbara, her faded brown hair in a tousle, standing in the center. when the older woman turned and saw her, an expression of fear flashed across her mild features, and she made a halting motion with her hands. the crowd paused, and let her through. barbara strode briskly to the olive-skinned girl, whose black hair, still frizzy from sleep, now seemed to stand straight up. they regarded one another, one anxiously, the other, fearfully. "what," barbara asked, lips white with tension, "did you do to margaret?"

what? it was almost a whisper. it had not occurred to her that, since she had returned to her own body, the body she had left might still exist somewhere else, shrouded by the inevitability of its death. *if death was a time of its own, perhaps zomia was the clock*, she thought. she was simply moving in the time of death. and then she fainted.

when she came to, the only thing she could see was bright, pulsing red all around her. she couldn't feel her legs, and

when she tried to move her arms, a spurt of intense red seemed to solidify around her eyes. she felt herself sliding, sliding . . . and then, pure white.

she had read, somewhere (was it baudrillard? the mouth of her professor? someone wiser than she) that writing could not be one's sole means of mediating herself. it produced self-indulgence, the likes of which we have not seen since the feminist modernists rotted into the banalities of white women's feeling poetry, or, a kind of arrogant lonely girl phenomenology, that is, finally, the confessional. sylvia plath might be one exception, but the majority of this Canon, which defined a hunk of "women's writing" and "contemporary womanhood" and "disrupting a phallocentric economy is a step toward female subjectivization (finally!)" seemed to her full of linguistic richness but with little function as political objects. and political objects they must be, with a service toward material (un)realities that ruptured the cultural institution of white supremacy.

case study: the unsuccessful readings of *the woman warrior* as autobiography, ethnography, creative nonfiction, all of which finally failed to trap maxine hong kingston within the realm of the truthful. the immigrant child is orphaned, once more, her feelings existing only as alienated text. knowing that anything she produced would be subject to rude white hands who attempted disassembly in place of comprehension, maxine hong kingston made no attempt of disclosure. so that her words could not be distorted against her, she wrote within the margins of the Narrative, eschewing names whilst claiming the ironically intimate first person until, finally, she had obfuscated authorial position so that only the tryptic of name remained. but initial readers, unable to segment *why this narrative even mattered*, had read it as if it were written in the first person autobiographical, entering maxine hong kingston into the circulation of a white discursive economy wherein text forcibly lined the boundaries of the body, and she mattered only because she had painted a harrowing portrait of Her Chinese Girlhood Filled With Subjective Chasms, from which point on became The Subjective Chasms of Chinese Girlhood, or pathetic chinese girl phenomenology. here's where the realm of the representational ended, and perhaps why ! felt, despite the openness of the grey sky, still hopelessly tethered to the window's rusted chains. for it wasn't enough to see shadows of herself in a literalization of *the woman warrior*—how could it come to be, that, in naming an archive of traumas, maxine hong kingston's text became emblematic of every chinese girl's trauma, a mythopoetic legibility that read similarly to the curious eyes of white murderers and lovers alike.

when chris kraus named The Dick to write a radical confessional of the Desiring Woman, she transcended the pettiness of individuality to achieve a categorical claim: the lonely girl phenomenology. or, She's Independent and Her Feelings Matter! but the lonely girl, despite the tragedies of her solitude, was in fact far from alone: there was an entire genealogy of them, driven by the radical assertion of their ego, whose Feelings All Mattered, and who would be listened to, despite, or because of their fluid navigation of categorical and individual concerns. white women could be both hopelessly narcissistic and still deny the representational burden. and through it all, she remains steadfastly capable of being heard, her utterance bearing not only the power of broadcast, but a specific naming mechanism that captured and indicted the object of wrath within endless strings of rambling, repurposed as nooses and cuffs. but when maxine hong kingston did the unthinkable by uttering some mythological secret that metonymized racialized pain, the only fruits of the trap were asian/

american women, whose representational scarcity rendered their individuated subjectivity a question to begin with. try as they might, they would only be listened to As A Group, interiorities elided into a monolith of sameness. so, try as she might, ! felt framed by the particular unfairness of the circumstances, wherein the freedom she felt was distinctly alienated from the freedom she could manifest, language being a manipulative contraption that, in mediating some poetry of interiority, sought to strap her to the operating table.

"let the atrocious images haunt us."

(susan sontag, *on photography*)

would it be that one day, someone might look at her photograph and envision a loss? and, more importantly, was such loss warranted, or did she feel it worthy of enactment from deep within the casket? ghosts were sentimental beings, she felt—otherwise, why did they always hold onto grudges of the flesh? but in the vast realm of the afterlife, when all became reduced to groundlings—there, would such petty concerns as nostalgia and regret find space to blossom? a few days before, she talked with her friend from college, a buoyant C, who was still trapped in the hinterlands of the campus (quite literally, for it was snowing with a fury designated especially for the fool's spring). between puffs of smoke (for what was a call without the actual *being togetherness* warranted by a hit?), they reminisced about the ludic warmth of los angeles, a location that was, though not equidistant between them, unreachable by either. yet it remained in the holding space of their imaginations, a place where they might be together under the sun. how funny, that to cope with the hollow isolation of williamstown (or any of its snowy cousins, like the northern european city in which she found herself), one had to evict herself from the actuality of place and love, elsewhere—that is, within the confines of the imaginary. but could it ever be reached? the real challenge was surviving the distance.

she had once dreamt about europe, attached to it the same significatory task of being the Unreached Place, for she dreamt of being in europe as an empty receptor, open to all the inspirations of the great continent. but she refused to be filled. or, it was that europe refused to fill her flask: she was not to suckle from its nipple, nor to take nutrition from the expanse of its knotted corpse. so los angeles— could it be a place whose familiarity protected her from the disappointments of idealization? as a child, she had spent many snot-filled summers in the calabasas suburbs, a fact that secured the city of angels as a place synonymous with childhood reverie, holy in the simple happiness it granted to her at one time. when she returned, after the stretch of a decade, she was surprised to find it still ripe with the treasures of folly. she created, in turn, sun-toned bodies under the waves. a sweet, albeit delirious, Time. this was not the los angeles to which she now longed to return, a vision of play trapped in the indulgences of growing blues.

an exhibition on van gogh's japonisme sea of blues—a comfort with which she desired to outline her own melancholy. the blue: a refuge from freudian shores' pull of excavation and resolution. but oh, blue was the color of the ocean, from whom she was now impossibly far. the prospect of touch—drowning, its most intimate iteration (couldn't ms. pontellier testify?)—impossible, too, in its queer fascination. where she was now: the laundromat off rue leopold the first, as close to the shore as she could get, though the ghost of the brutal belgian king hunched between dock and mast. the laundromat possessed an incomprehensible payment machine, which produced a series of comical exchanges: confused patrons being aided by more experienced visitors still trapped in the fish tank, waiting for their load. she was helped by a frail woman, who guided her in french and offered a detergent pod from her own box when the vending machine broke. later, two middle-aged men, clad in slippers and jeans, colonial french spilling from their tongues with more fragrance than the original text offered. she felt comforted in their midst, as if returned to the laundromats of her youth, places similarly frequented by ladies in solid-colored burkas and older men in polyester sweatpants, the likes of which her father owned in endless quality.

the first laundromat she could remember was located on the steep incline of a hill. from the stoop of its entrance, one could see the shoreline, and, on clear days, the dimming horizon of the sun, whose golden flask spilled onto vertical shadows as they crouched under the weight of the heaving basket. when she thought of it, she envisioned a loss, though there was nothing tangible to lose. a pair of stockings, perhaps, or a mismatched sock, but the visual residue of the Place—and truly, it could have been a number of Places—remained grief-worthy in her mind, a moment she would have liked to scrutinize under the dim lights of a coffee shop. but immigrants do not open cafés—perhaps they did, in their home countries, but when faced with the precarity of deracination, who had time for the idleness of coffee? someone paid for the luxury of leisure, and it could not be them, who were stuck in their ateliers and restaurants, endless mini-marts and corner bodegas. the cost of sitting was high, so everybody stood, even the ghosts, until they floated away, leaving shadows only visible in the dusk.

another letter to ! (editor's note: undated)

she was long gone now, he was sure of that. but as he watched the scratchy surveillance video, he could not help but wonder at the impossibility of that statement. how could she be *gone*, when even the visage of her, transmitted over the weak feed of the pixels, could convince him that she was here, next to him? the tape had been backlogged; as a result, he was the first to view it. all the crucial evidence had been dissected in the limelight—there was little possibility that this footage, a chance documentation of her wanderings in a little town of côte d'azur, could reveal anything that was not already known. but he watched, as he had always done, when an image of her appeared. he found that in her absence, the vivacity which she had once conveyed heightened, until it was as if she were still alive. as in this video, which transmuted all other incidents, imposing her liveliness onto the ruined fabric of the present.

it was a quiet night. the street was dimly lit, but passersby strolled with ease, some alone, most accompanied by the warmth of another. she stood alone, lighting a cigarette on the corner of a plaza, then stuffed her hands into her pockets, and marched (yes, she had always marched) onto the cobbled sidewalk. there were a disproportionate number of police that night. they gathered in groups at the ends of streets, threatening to spill over into oncoming traffic. she looked this way and that, perhaps curiously peered at the uniformed men and women, as he had known her often to do. she never threatened the police; at most, one would nod politely to her, and she might scowl in return, then hunch her long torso and hurry past them. tonight, there were no such interactions, but, as she passed the car, a swarm of people with bouquets rushed past her. for a second, she was lost among the crowd, a dot of black amongst a cascade of tiny blossoms. when she appeared again, it was at the edge of the crowd. she was scribbling something in a notebook, cigarette dangling from the side of her mouth. police and people with flowers, he imagined her writing. she would have found something poetic about such an event; poetic, despite and perhaps because of, its incongruous violence.

once, when he was going through the endless collection of her papers, he had discovered a slip tucked within her favorite copy of *the political unconscious*. the chapter had been on balzac, and she had scribbled, in her slight hand, "to be in the presence of police—althusser—she would write in lieu of an idea (pretending, even in writing)." times like these made him miss her more than ever, for it was not just her he missed, but all of her invisible interlocutors, her internal monologue, the chaos that was her grand autobiographical narration. her schizophrenic raznorechie, she liked to call it. now there was no more. or, now that was all there was.

the street that night was surprisingly quiet. he noted a sense of disequilibrium: so few people, so many weapons. even their state of california, with its multiple contingency units, rarely saw such action. he wondered if she had thought of home in that moment. he wondered if home was ever in her thoughts, even now. she walked briskly into a fast-food joint—here, he swiveled to find the tape inside the store, and played it in real time with the footage of the street. with much trepidation, she ordered a cheese and egg taco, articulating her order to a very pretty but confused french waiter, whose pink lips puckered when she uttered (or, so he thought), "you know salade?" her soft body twisted this way and that—no doubt ! also found her charming. she had always felt, she said to him, trapped between adoration and emulation of such easy femininity. but i'm not easy, she concluded. i'm cracked.

in her journal entry, she, too, had written of that day in the third person, as if she had decided, then and there, that her centrality was no longer. *suddenly, she began to feel dizzy, her eyes very tired and very small. her hair, what waft of it was left, made her as she had never wished to become. she felt a queer experiment, gone wrong. thirsty. she found the diet coke she had hoarded earlier. where was the bathroom?* she was redefining "travel/ writing" (here, he felt her laughing ironically) *by entrapping it within the momentary, the literary. but weren't we always already traveling? all the time, here to there to there and maybe back to here and—so on. all writing is, by nature, travel/writing.*

oh, how he wished he could travel to her now, wherever she might be. they could make light of anything—even the bottom of the ocean, which he felt sure (he calculated bitterly) was where she now floated. the last memory he had of her: at the train station, her suitcase abandoned, as she gesticulated furiously, *did you see that, over there, the man carrying on his shoulders a little girl with a neon green clown wig?* they had laughed together, he urging her to hurry, she promising to write—to him, this incident, every incident which made her feel as if he were with her. with a flurry of a kiss (which she tried to extend, before he pulled away), she was gone.

diary entries (editor's note: undated)

i woke, under plank of arm shuddering with the still-blue of dawn, petulant with remorse and angry with the letter "h." he looked at me, eyes fluttering with the dim light of sleep, and reached over to stroke my waist. i let his hand linger. breathed warm exhaust on the slight curve of his chin, and wondered if [redacted], five years trapped in the period of the love story, had finally broken free. metafictions, told to myself: once, there was a traitor. i have always hated the words: priapic, bildungsroman. if his breathing slowed, and i puckered my lips, might we bite away the vines of the next morning? i am here to make a mockery of the bildungsroman, i thought to myself, as he nibbled on my neck. but when i looked over, the story was nowhere to be found, and bodies, heavy with the aroma of cigarettes, lay strewn about the room. the weight of my body, sinking to the ground: what is erotica, in the absence of air? what is the love story, cleaved from its page by the moan of the comma. i have never known the love story, or, i have always felt its ghost. hauntological signs and an impossible future, his words drive me dizzy and i close my eyes, draw the sentences close, and try to sleep. dark sleep, between foreign limbs and the pretense of warmth—i have been betrothed to the gestures of intimacy, now i cower in their obsolescence.

question: if you loved him, and he might love you too, could you blow air to dispel all possibility of reunion? they say you were born with an invisible thread tied to your finger, and through the travails of life, the unknotting leads you to your intended. my intent: to escape. the knots: tied by cartilage, deported from the shadow of the warmth. i do not love him, but my body leaking air and wet mucus trace the length of his spine and lie crooked in the nape of his chest. on the stage of fucking, there are no prisoners, only deportees looking over the horizon of the dusk. click, the dark sleep, and we roam lost terrain with the tenacity of the starved. it is possible to confuse the stick for the carrot, and in this case, i'm afraid i've eaten it, plank, peel, and all.

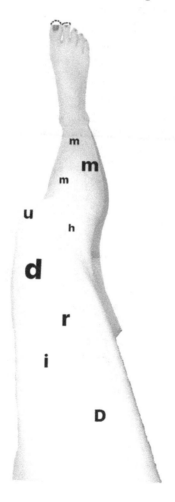

was this the last thing she would write? when did the end begin, and slowly engulf the capacity for reproduction. she was not made to reproduce, her organs cracked and made dry by decades in the desert. where others had lush greens and the anticipatory musk of fertile plains, her gates enclosed an everlasting drought. parched, so others don't have to be—so she told herself, through gritted nubs papered by years of sand. she had read somewhere that it was best to poach her life on either side of the extreme: specialize and expertize, or fail, and commit to the flail, which is to say, there is no scale or hierarchy or metonym for measurement, only commitment. perseverance in her capacity, a kind of fearlessness. but what if she failed to possess the capacity needed for excellence? or could not ground her already stumpy ambition to embers in the ground? she felt the pull of mediocrity, which was in truth a swinging motion offset by the occasional wink of potential. she would always be a deflowered virgin, though she hid her hesitance and reeling surprise with a facade of confidence disguised as speed. always on the move—people took it for competence, and she harvested this quality despite the drag of her sloping left shoulder, an inch too close to the ground.

she could not remember the precise timing of the ache. pulsing, with no intention of relent, the knot (or was it a bruise?) was ignored, and, when it could no longer be ignored, accepted. some time ago, she had received a massage from a lover, who, unsatisfied with the contortions of copulation, had asked to twist her limbs in the aftermath of the act. they took turns kneading the ropy muscles of the other's body, touching with a sensitivity they had forgotten while locked in embrace. she had not liked the massage, but she thought about it often, how under the caress of another she had turned and offered her lips to be kissed, then penetrated. how she could recall such scenes so vividly; that she could render them written with explosive eroticism—all of this had terrified her. the smell of her lover, too, terrified her, for the imprecision of their act satisfied, but only under the contract of impermanence—so she must always already have forgotten, always already be on the run. but the taste of her lover would not fade despite the unfiltered cigarettes she drank to pause it all.

in her day, she had taken her fair share of admirers, though none had stuck (an irony at which she laughed silently, immobilized by her sticky joints). the curse of solitude might have been due to her empty fifth house, a feat by the stars which promised that she would never break free from the orbit of temporary touches, the planet of ill-fated single encounters. for this reason, among others, she had trouble leaving places, and everything she touched grew tentacles which arose to attach themselves around her. things came easily, but they seldom contained a timely stay, so that she found herself surrounded by heaps of accidental clutter, unsure where or how they had arrived, in the sprained chamber of her clavicle. the stains would not rub out. no matter how much she threw away, she always came back to more: hidden in the crevice of the wall, between soiled blankets, beneath the ratty carpet, and even—she discovered one day—in the space between her eyes, where they had eaten cartilage until all that remained was the hollow shell of bone.

Acknowledgements

Though my life, and the lives of !, S, and this book are now wedded in print, neither S, !, nor I could have accomplished the task of its (our) birth alone.

This book would not exist were it not for the encouragement of Professor Dorothy Wang. Professor Wang, for your endless integrity, wisdom, and generosity, there are not enough words. S is sharper because of your guidance, and I am braver because of your care. This book is for you.

I remain permanently indebted to my parents, Joan Zhang (章智红) and Xander Tang (唐先南), without whose love and labor neither S nor I would have survived. Mama and Baba, I love you. This book is as much yours as it is mine.

It is both a joy and a dream come true to have gotten to work with Janice Lee at The Accomplices. To Janice, Devyn, Esa, and the team at The Accomplices, thank you for your careful eyes, gentle notes, and for allowing me to join a roster of excellent company. We're coping; we're thriving.

For my chosen family, near and far: Dawn, Calen, Tyler, Olivia, Audrey, Linda, Eman, Wei Jie and so many others. This book lives for and because of you.

Lastly, to the writers and texts referenced implicitly and explicitly throughout:

Pamela Lu, *Pamela: A Novel* / Eunsong Kim, *Gospel of Regicide* Chris Kraus, *Aliens and Anorexia; I Love Dick; Topor* / Amanda Lee Koe, *Ministry of Moral Panics* / Carmen Maria Machado, *Her Body and Other Parties* / Dorothy Wang, *Thinking Its Presence: Form, Race, and Subjectivity in Contemporary Asian American Poetry* / Christina Sharpe, In the Wake: *On Blackness and Being* / Eugene Lim, *Dear Cyborgs: A Novel* / erin Khuê Ninh, *Ingratitude: The Debt-Bound Daughter of Asian American Literature* / Anne Anlin Cheng, *The Melancholy of Race: Psychoanalysis, Assimilation, and Hidden Race* / Tao Lin, *Bed: Stories* / Nella Larsen, *Passing* / Chang Rae Lee, *Native Speaker* / Anaïs Nin, ed. Gunther Stuhlmann *Diary of Anïs Nin, Vol. 1* / Susan Sontag, ed. David Rieff *On Photography; Reborn: Journals and Notebooks, 1947-1963*

OFFICIAL

THE ACCOMPLICES

GET OUT OF JAIL
* VOUCHER *

- -

Tear this out.

Skip that social event.

It's okay.

You don't have to go if you don't want to. Pick up the book you just bought. Open to the first page.

You'll thank us by the third paragraph.

If friends ask why you were a no-show, show them this voucher.

You'll be fine.

- -

We're thriving.

CPSIA information can be obtained
at www.ICGtesting.com
Printed in the USA
LVHW090339251019
635310LV00001B/145/P

9 781948 700986